Sanditon

Jane Austen

ET REMOTISSIMA PROPE

Hesperus Classics

Hesperus Classics
Published by Hesperus Press Limited
4 Rickett Street, London sw6 1ru
www.hesperuspress.com

First published in 1925
First published by Hesperus Press Limited, 2009

Foreword © A.C. Grayling, 2009

Designed and typeset by Fraser Muggeridge studio
Printed in Jordan by Al-Khayyam Printing Press

ISBN: 978-1-84391-184-5

CONTENTS

FOREWORD

Sanditon was the last of Jane Austen's fictional works. She began writing it on 27th January 1817, and ceased work on it just under two months later, on 18th March, part of the way through the twelfth chapter. She died a mere four months after that, on 18th July 1817, aged forty-two. It is thought that she died of Addison's disease, a disorder of the adrenal glands often secondary to tuberculosis. In light of one of the main themes of *Sanditon*, namely illness or supposed illness, it is relevant that the symptoms of this once-fatal disease begin by being consistent with hypochondria, only after a while becoming evidence of serious decay. Addison's is a rare condition in which the adrenal glands produce insufficient natural steroids, with the result that the body cannot cope with inflammation. Its symptoms are exhaustion, weakness, feelings of faintness on standing up, headaches, backache – and these of course could be mere 'vapours' produced by lack of exercise and over-eating, or by nervous sensibility, or the onset of menopause.

But then the disease progresses to vomiting and diarrhoea, sweating, weight loss, salt cravings, painful joints, and marked personality change. Evidently Jane Austen was using – and satirising – as material for her novel what in the earlier phase of her illness she perhaps thought were her own 'vapours', along with the then increasing barrage of advertisements for seaside health cures. And alas, what she robustly mistook for something that common sense would help her survive was, instead, the harbinger of death. It makes the theme of imaginary ill health in *Sanditon* all the more poignant and telling.

It is a tragedy that literary genius of Jane Austen's proportions should have had so little time to express itself. Although she began to write early, completing what came to be called

Sense and Sensibility and *Pride and Prejudice* in the 1790s, they were not published until 1811 and 1813 respectively. So Austen's career as a published author was very short – a mere six years, in which her sense of her powers as a writer was confirmed both by the critical and financial success of her work, and her own creative outpouring: *Mansfield Park* was begun in 1811 as *Sense and Sensibility* was first appearing on the booksellers' shelves, and as soon as it was finished in 1813, with *Pride and Prejudice* just being published, she began *Emma*, finishing it a year later (it was published in 1815) and immediately starting *Persuasion*, which was completed in the autumn of 1816. From the fact that she set to work on *Sanditon* just a few months later, at the beginning of 1817, it is clear that she was on what we nowadays called 'a roll', and an extra-ordinary one. It is a loss merely to imagine what else her increasingly prolific gift might have produced had she lived.

Jane Austen made her will on 27th April 1817, at last suspecting or acknowledging that she was seriously ill. She had both *Persuasion* and *Northanger Abbey* – the latter written long before, several times offered to publishers without success, and revised and renamed more than once – in press during that summer, so it is easy to imagine how pregnant with work she must have felt, and aware of how cruelly she was being cut short in the midst of her gifts.

Add to this the signs in *Sanditon* that something a little new was entering Jane Austen's vintage style and concerns – on this, more below – and the poignancy of her loss to literature is complete: she had so much more to do and say, and she was moving with the times when her time ran out.

It is tempting to describe *Sanditon* as simultaneously the most modern and the most eighteenth century of all Jane Austen's fictions. It is eighteenth century in aspects of its language, most notably the frequency of balanced periods reminiscent of the styles of Dr Johnson and Edward Gibbon. For three examples: Sanditon is economically described as a seaside town 'the most favoured by nature, and promising to be the most chosen by man'; the character of the life enjoyed by Mr and Mrs Heywood is conveyed in the words, 'What prudence had first enjoined, was now rendered pleasant by habit'; Lady Denham tells a friend, 'though she had got nothing but her title from the family, still she had given nothing for it'. The economy and authority of these literary mannerisms, quite consciously employed, were doubtless an enjoyment to Austen; she knew they would be recognised and equally enjoyed by people who, like herself, had cut their reader's teeth on the novels, essays and poetry of the eighteenth century in which they had been young. The manner is not new in her writing, but in this fragment it appears more deliberate, as if to point the irony felt by the author in her commentary on the new world she describes.

Sanditon is also eighteenth century in its reliance on letters, reminding one of *Lady Susan*, Jane Austen's first fictional work, wholly written in epistolary style after the manner of the author who was her greatest inspiration, Samuel Richardson. Although only a short fragment, *Sanditon* already contains the reading aloud of two important letters and seventeen others reported between the characters; no doubt plenty more – both mentioned and read aloud – would have been called into service of the plot. Only think: Sidney Parker – surely destined to propose to Charlotte on the last page – is first met with as he passes through Sanditon on his way to the Isle of Wight. He must write to his family from there. He is expecting the company of 'one or two' friends, one of them, surely, destined to have something to do with Clara Brereton: more letters loom. Diana Parker and her supposedly ailing siblings are due to return to London in a week, whither and whence more letters of interest to Charlotte, Sidney and others must flow. And at whatever point Charlotte returns to her family at Willingden, perhaps by then under the sad misapprehension that Clara (or perhaps the West Indian heiress Miss Lambe?) is the object of Sidney's affections, she would be in need of many letters to keep track of affairs. How else, for example, would she (and we) know the progress of Sir Edward Denham's relations first with Clara and then, surely, with Miss Lambe also? How would she know what Sidney had written to his siblings in London and his brother in Sanditon? How would she know what Lady Denham was proposing with respect to her will?

I repeat 'surely' so often because of course one cannot be sure what would transpire from the characters and circumstances so richly and promisingly assembled in the first twelve chapters of *Sanditon*. As Jane Austen fans we can make these guesses, and probably be more right than wrong; but there is the intriguing matter of something new in this novel, a hint that just as the world had moved on now that the long and exhausting war with France was over, so had Jane Austen herself.

And this brings us to the reason why *Sanditon* is the most modern of her writings. It is decidedly a post-war work, the new fashions and preoccupations of the world after Waterloo providing its background. Sanditon is a small seaside town whose two principal residents, the eldest Mr Parker and Lady Denham, are keen to make it a fashionable resort after the manner of others then growing in size and importance along the coasts of England. The medicinal properties of sea bathing and sea air had been a late eighteenth-century discovery, and the Prince Regent's Pavilion at Brighton had put the seal of fashion on the gradual switch from spa resorts (Bath was the most fashionable but not the only one) to the seaside. For Jane Austen the rapid commercial growth of seaside resorts, the blurring of class lines (at Sanditon a commercially minded member of the minor gentry is on equal terms with a baronet and his father's dowager), the abandonment of a snug house in a valley some miles from the sea in favour of a cliff-top new house exposed to the ocean's blasts, are all matters for comment, not all of it unfavourable. The hill and cliff at Sanditon have a new row of terraced houses built over them, and a paved promenade; this is today's world, not the world of *Pride and Prejudice* or *Emma*. Mr Parker and Lady Denham discuss their rents from the letting of summer lodgings; we are a thousand miles from Sir Walter Elliot of Kellynch Hall, though even he had to become a rentier to survive: but how differently it all feels in Sir Walter's world – what a different kind of baronet he is.

Moreover, there is the manner in which *Sanditon* combines its modernity and its eighteenth century-ness: the strikingly frank way it addresses the question of sexual morality. Sir Edward Denham, under the influence of Richardson's Lovelace, wishes to set himself up as a seducer. Jane Austen tells us quite explicitly that he plots the ruin of Clara, the poor relation of his stepmother Lady Denham. He has a practical motive too: he needs to inherit Lady Denham's great wealth, because he is too poor for his station in life, and he is worried that she might leave her money to Clara. Therefore ruining her is a means of getting her out of the way. We are not told in these twelve too-brief chapters, but we might wonder, whether the alternative – namely, Sir Edward marrying Clara – was not open to him because of the disparity of their stations in life, and the fact that she was poor, there being no guarantee that Lady Denham would leave her much.

Sir Edward, then, is not a seducer quite like *Sense and Sensibility's* Willoughby or *Pride and Prejudice's* Wickham, but someone for whom – quite explicitly – despoiling a young woman is a planned option, even if in a rather hazy, not to say silly, gothic envisioning, which involves carrying Clara off to a cottage near Timbuctoo. True, Willoughby seduced Colonel Brandon's ward Eliza and left her pregnant, but this is reported at a distance in *Sense and Sensibility*, not brought to the front of the stage as in *Sanditon*; and it is also true that Willoughby really loved Marianne and learns too late that he could have behaved with honour all along, and gained both her and his inheritance; but the stain of moral crime, in the universe of Austen's published novels, typically derails individual lives, so we cannot be sure what fate awaits Sir Edward Denham for all that there is more both of the Lovelace and the popinjay in him than in either Willoughby or Wickham.

The morality play promised by Sir Edward's thoughts is just one of the strands projected in the novel, as hypochondria and self-indulgence is another. But the real key to *Sanditon* lies in the fact that Jane Austen at first contemplated calling it *The Brothers* – meaning of course the three Parker brothers. The eldest is the good-natured, somewhat obsessive commercial developer of Sanditon, the youngest is the good-natured, fat, self-coddling, over-eating young man who lives with his sisters and will not contemplate an active and useful life. Chief of the three is the middle brother Sidney, obviously intended to be *Sanditon's* hero, who will assuredly roll Darcy, Colonel Brandon and Mr Knightley into one (there is less in what we hear of him of Edward Ferrars or Edmund Bertram – that is, the quiet moral type). He will rescue Clara, aid Miss Lambe, be of service to the Heywoods in some way, and at last marry Charlotte – perhaps after helping her to correct her primness, rather as Mr Knightley helped Emma correct her meddlings, misperceptions and insensitivities.

The contrast between the brothers, the differences evident in their actions and fates as a result of the differences in their characters, therefore appears to be the major theme of *Sanditon*, and the rich palette of other characters and possibilities already apparent in the twelve chapters is clearly intended to paint these differences in vivid colours.

Sidney is well off, well bred, intelligent and witty, full of common sense, a traveller, an active and affectionate man – his relationship to his family and their fond reports of him show all this already. In this respect Sidney is portrayed as most of the characters in Austen's published novels are portrayed: by being talked about, or shown in action. A big difference between *Sanditon* and Austen's published novels is that so many of the characters are directly described; we are *told*, rather than *shown*, what their characters are. The languishing Lady Bertram, the valetudinarian Mr Woodhouse, the scatter-brained younger Bennett sisters, the proud Mr Darcy, the cheerful Mr Bingham, his unpleasantly artful sisters, the snobbish Lady Catherine, the oleaginous Mr Collins, the overwrought Marianne, the shrinking Fanny, the interesting and slightly dangerous Miss Crawford, are revealed to us by what they do and say, and by what others say. In *Sanditon* the majority of the characters are not revealed to us in this way; rather, we are given direct particulars of them, almost as if we were reading Austen's own character sketches for them from her planning papers.

True, both Sir Edward and Lady Denham do some of the work for themselves in showing us what they are, as does

Diane Parker. And so too of course does Charlotte, though as the observing authorial presence in what is just an opening section she has yet to show more of herself; so far she is most like Elizabeth Bennett, observant, down to earth, her cleverness and strength tempered by extremely good manners – but she also has a tincture of Fanny in her primness: witness how she turns the conversation to the weather when Sir Edward broaches the subject of how woman's beauty prompts the male of the species to forego morality.

But these, with Sidney, are the exceptions. This is really a large difference of approach from the other novels, and it gives one pause for thought. I think Austen takes the tack of direct portrayal for a reason, namely, that the plot promises to be more complex, with more twists and turns, and with more players directly involved in the confusions and unhappiness that must presage resolution, so that a far more detailed working out is required. In the published novels the leisurely unfolding of character by showing rather than telling is a large part of the point of each book. Here – so one guesses – with so many fully developed actors on stage or just about to make their entrances, less room is given to character development so that there can be more room for events, for emotions to be roused and doused, and for the comedy of the situation to support the threat of tragedy, which we happily expect to be averted and resolved to general satisfaction.

Jane Austen was a careful plotter of her novels, which are dramas of feeling and the way feelings relate to the delicate tissue of moral justice. This relation works aright if the feelings in question are rational (in both senses of proportionate and thoughtful). The most explicit working out of this proposition occurs in *Sense and Sensibility*, but it is the philosophical underpinning of all her work. So for example: there would not be mention of the snug house in the valley where the Parkers used to live unless its role in the economy of the novel is significant – not just as a contrast to the Parkers' weather-exposed new villa on the cliff top, but perhaps where Charlotte and Sidney might settle after marriage; or perhaps, at very least, as a topic of conversation between them, in which Sidney can show his preference for the sensibly placed mature old house with its shelter and comforts as against the brash new world so ardently welcomed by his older brother.

Every thread-end presented in these twelve chapters, in short, is a promissory note for the complexities to come, and there are so many of them – more than in any of the published novels – and there are so many fully drawn characters, that the notion here suggested, that this would have been a more complex and perhaps a longer novel than its predecessors, makes its own case.

This suggestion, if correct, must add to our regret that *Sanditon* stands unfinished, mouth-wateringly and tragically so. It explains why there have been so many efforts by other hands to finish the story; it cries out to continue, it begs for development and a denouement. I persist in thinking *Sanditon* would have turned out to be a larger piece of ivory than any yet inscribed by Austen. The failure of efforts by others to continue the tale is proof, if proof were needed, that only Jane Austen's genius could properly finish what the *Sanditon* fragment begins. As it is, we have only our imaginations, and the rest of her works, to suggest to us what the treasury of the tale might look like if it were not locked away forever behind the doors of death.

– A.C. Grayling, 2009

Sanditon

CHAPTER ONE

A gentleman and lady travelling from Tunbridge towards that part of the Sussex coast which lies between Hastings and Eastbourne, being induced by business to quit the high road and attempt a very rough lane, were overturned in toiling up its long ascent, half rock, half sand. The accident happened just beyond the only gentleman's house near the lane, a house which their driver, on being first required to take that direction, had conceived to be necessarily their object and had with most unwilling looks been constrained to pass by. He had grumbled and shaken his shoulders and pitied and cut his horses so sharply that he might have been open to the suspicion of overturning them on purpose (especially as the carriage was not his master's own) if the road had not indisputably become worse than before, as soon as the premises of the said house were left behind, expressing with a most portentous countenance that, beyond it, no wheels but cart wheels could safely proceed. The severity of the fall was broken by their slow pace and the narrowness of the lane, and the gentleman having scrambled out and helped out his companion, they neither of them at first felt more than shaken and bruised. But the gentleman had, in the course of the extrication, sprained his foot, and soon becoming sensible of it, was obliged in a few moments to cut short both his remonstrance to the driver and his congratulations to his wife and himself and sit down on the bank, unable to stand.

'There is something wrong here,' said he, putting his hand to his ankle. 'But never mind, my dear,' looking up at her with a smile, 'it could not have happened, you know, in a better place. Good out of evil. The very thing perhaps to be wished for. We shall soon get relief. There, I fancy, lies my cure,' he said, pointing to the neat-looking end of a cottage, which was seen romantically situated among wood on a high eminence at some little distance. 'Does not *that* promise to be the very place?'

His wife fervently hoped it was, but stood, terrified and anxious, neither able to do or suggest anything, and receiving her first real comfort from the sight of several persons now coming to their assistance. The accident had been discerned from a hayfield adjoining the house they had passed, and the persons who approached were a well-looking, hale, gentlemanlike man of middle age, the proprietor of the place, who happened to be among his haymakers at the time, and three or four of the ablest of them summoned to attend their master, to say nothing of all the rest of the field, men, women and children, not very far off. Mr Heywood, such was the name of the said proprietor, advanced with a very civil salutation, much concern for the accident, some surprise at anybody's attempting that road in a carriage, and ready offers of assistance. His courtesies were received with good breeding and gratitude, and while one or two of the men lent their help to the driver in getting the carriage upright again, the traveller said, 'You are extremely obliging, sir, and I take you at your word. The injury to my leg is, I dare say, very trifling. But it is always best in these cases, you know, to have a surgeon's opinion without loss of time, and as the road does not seem in a favourable state for my getting up to his house myself, I will thank you to send off one of these good people for the surgeon.'

'The surgeon, sir!' exclaimed Mr Heywood. 'I am afraid you will find no surgeon at hand here, but I dare say we shall do very well without him.'

'Nay sir, if he is not in the way, his partner will do just as well, or rather better. I would rather see his partner indeed. I would prefer the attendance of his partner. One of these good people can be with him in three minutes, I am sure. I need not ask whether I see the house,' looking towards the cottage, 'for excepting your own, we have passed none in this place which can be the abode of a gentleman.'

Mr Heywood looked very much astonished. 'What, sir! Are you expecting to find a surgeon in that cottage? We have neither surgeon nor partner in the parish, I assure you.'

'Excuse me, sir,' replied the other. 'I am sorry to have the appearance of contradicting you, but from the extent of the parish or some other cause you may not be aware of the fact, stay! Can I be mistaken in the place? Am I not in Willingden? Is not this Willingden?'

'Yes, sir, this is certainly Willingden.'

'Then, sir, I can bring proof of your having a surgeon in the parish, whether you may know it or not. Here, sir,' (taking out his pocket book), 'if you will do me the favour of casting your eye over these advertisements which I cut out myself from the *Morning Post* and the *Kentish Gazette* only yesterday morning in London, I think you will be convinced that I am not speaking at random. You will find in it an advertisement of the dissolution of a partnership in the medical line, in your own parish, extensive business, undeniable character, respectable references, wishing to form a separate establishment. You will find it at full length, sir,' offering the two little oblong extracts.

'Sir,' said Mr Heywood with a good-humoured smile, 'if you were to show me all the newspapers that are printed in one week throughout the kingdom, you would not persuade me of there being a surgeon in Willingden, for having lived here ever since I was born, man and boy fifty-seven years, I think I must have known of such a person. At least I may venture to say that he has not much business. To be sure, if gentlemen were to be often attempting this lane in post-chaises, it might not be a bad speculation for a surgeon to get a house at the top of the hill. But as to that cottage, I can assure you, sir, that it is in fact, in spite of its spruce air at this distance, as indifferent a double tenement as any in the parish, and that my shepherd lives at one end and three old women at the other.' He took the pieces of paper as he spoke, and, having looked them over, added, 'I believe I can explain it, sir. Your mistake *is* in the place. There are two Willingdens in this country. Your advertisements must refer to the other, which is Great Willingden or Willingden Abbots, and lies seven miles off on the other side of Battel, quite down in the weald. And we, sir,' he added, speaking rather proudly, 'are not in the weald.'

'Not down in the weald, I am sure,' replied the traveller pleasantly. 'It took us half an hour to climb your hill. Well sir, I dare say it is as you say and I have made an abominably stupid blunder. All done in a moment, the advertisements did not catch my eye until the last half hour of our being in town, everything in the hurry and confusion which always attend a short stay there. One is never able to complete anything in the way of business, you know, until the carriage is at the door, and accordingly satisfying myself with a brief enquiry, and finding we were actually to pass within a mile or two of a Willingden, I sought no farther. My dear,' (to his wife), 'I am very sorry to have brought you into this scrape. But do not be alarmed about my leg. It gives me no pain while I am quiet, and as soon as these good people have succeeded in setting the carriage to rights and turning the horses round, the best thing we can do will be to measure back our steps into the turnpike road and proceed to Hailsham, and so home, without attempting anything farther. Two hours take us home from Hailsham. And when once at home, we have our remedy at hand, you know. A little of our own bracing sea air will soon set me on my feet again. Depend upon it, my dear, it is exactly a case for the sea. Saline air and immersion will be the very thing. My sensations tell me so already.'

In a most friendly manner Mr Heywood here interposed, entreating them not to think of proceeding until the ankle had been examined and some refreshment taken, and very cordially pressing them to make use of his house for both purposes. 'We are always well stocked,' said he, 'with all the common remedies for sprains and bruises, and I will answer for the pleasure it will give my wife and daughters to be of service to you in every way in their power.'

A twinge or two, in trying to move his foot, disposed the traveller to think rather more than he had done at first of the benefit of immediate assistance; and consulting his wife in the few words of, 'Well, my dear, I believe it will be better for us,' he turned again to Mr Heywood. 'Before we accept your hospitality sir, and in order to do away with any unfavourable impression which the sort of wild-goose chase you find me in may have given rise to, allow me to tell you who we are. My name is Parker, Mr Parker of Sanditon; this lady, my wife, Mrs Parker. We are on our road home from London. My name perhaps, though I am by no means the first of my family holding landed property in the parish of Sanditon, may be unknown at this distance from the coast. But Sanditon itself, everybody has heard of Sanditon. The favourite, for a young and rising bathing place, certainly the favourite spot of all that are to be found along the coast of Sussex; the most favoured by nature, and promising to be the most chosen by man.'

'Yes, I have heard of Sanditon,' replied Mr Heywood. 'Every five years, one hears of some new place or other starting up by the sea and growing the fashion. How they can half of them be filled is the wonder! Where people can be found with money and time to go to them! Bad things for a country, sure to raise the price of provisions and make the poor good for nothing, as I dare say you find, sir.'

'Not at all, sir, not at all,' cried Mr Parker eagerly. 'Quite the contrary, I assure you. A common idea, but a mistaken one. It may apply to your large, overgrown places like Brighton or Worthing or Eastbourne, but not to a small village like Sanditon, precluded by its size from experiencing any of the evils of civilisation; while the growth of the place, the buildings, the nursery grounds, the demand for everything and the sure resort of the very best company, those regular, steady, private families of thorough gentility and character who are a blessing everywhere, excite the industry of the poor and diffuse comfort and improvement among them of every sort. No sir, I assure you, Sanditon is not a place –'

'I do not mean to take exception to any place in particular,' answered Mr Heywood. 'I only think our coast is too full of them altogether. But had we not better try to get you –'

'Our coast too full!' repeated Mr Parker. 'On that point perhaps we may not totally disagree. At least there are enough. Our coast is abundant enough. It demands no more. Everybody's taste and everybody's finances may be suited. And those good people who are trying to add to the number are, in my opinion, excessively absurd and must soon find themselves the dupes of their own fallacious calculations. Such a place as Sanditon, sir, I may say was wanted, was called for. Nature had marked it out, had spoken in most intelligible characters. The finest, purest sea breeze on the coast, acknowledged to be so, excellent bathing, fine hard sand, deep water ten yards from the shore, no mud, no weeds, no slimy rocks. Never was there a place more palpably designed by nature for the resort of the invalid, the very spot which thousands seemed in need of! The most desirable distance from London! One complete, measured mile nearer than Eastbourne. Only conceive, sir, the advantage of saving a whole mile in a long journey. But Brinshore, sir, which I dare say you have in your eye, the attempts of two or three speculating people about Brinshore this last year to raise that paltry hamlet, lying as it does between a stagnant marsh, a bleak moor and the constant effluvia of a ridge of putrefying seaweed, can end in nothing but their own disappointment. What in the name of common sense is to recommend Brinshore? A most insalubrious air, roads proverbially detestable, water brackish beyond example, impossible to get a good dish of tea within three miles of the place. And as for the soil, it is so cold and ungrateful that it can hardly be made to yield a cabbage. Depend upon it, sir, that this is a most faithful description of Brinshore, not in the smallest degree exaggerated, and if you have heard it differently spoken of –'

'Sir, I never heard it spoken of in my life before,' said Mr Heywood. 'I did not know there was such a place in the world.'

'You did not! There, my dear,' turning with exultation to his wife, 'you see how it is. So much for the celebrity of Brinshore! This gentleman did not know there was such a place in the world. Why, in truth, sir, I fancy we may apply to Brinshore that line of the poet Cowper in his description of the religious cottager, as opposed to Voltaire: "She, never heard of half a mile from home."'

'With all my heart, sir, apply any verses you like to it. But I want to see something applied to your leg. And I am sure by your lady's countenance that she is quite of my opinion and thinks it a pity to lose any more time. And here come my girls to speak for themselves and their mother.' Two or three genteel-looking young women, followed by as many maid servants, were now seen issuing from the house. 'I began to wonder the bustle should not have reached them. A thing of this kind soon makes a stir in a lonely place like ours. Now, sir, let us see how you can be best conveyed into the house.'

The young ladies approached and said everything that was proper to recommend their father's offers, and in an unaffected manner calculated to make the strangers easy. As Mrs Parker was exceedingly anxious for relief, and her husband by this time not much less disposed for it, a very few civil scruples were enough; especially as the carriage, being now set up, was discovered to have received such injury on the fallen side as to be unfit for present use. Mr Parker was therefore carried into the house and his carriage wheeled off to a vacant barn.

CHAPTER TWO

The acquaintance, thus oddly begun, was neither short nor unimportant. For a whole fortnight the travellers were fixed at Willingden, Mr Parker's sprain proving too serious for him to move sooner. He had fallen into very good hands. The Heywoods were a thoroughly respectable family and every possible attention was paid, in the kindest and most unpretending manner, to both husband and wife. He was waited on and nursed, and she cheered and comforted with unremitting kindness. As every office of hospitality and friendliness was received as it ought, as there was not more good will on one side than gratitude on the other, nor any deficiency of generally pleasant manners in either, they grew to like each other in the course of that fortnight exceedingly well.

Mr Parker's character and history were soon unfolded. All that he understood of himself, he readily told, for he was very openhearted; and where he might be himself in the dark, his conversation was still giving information to such of the Heywoods as could observe. By such he was perceived to be an enthusiast; on the subject of Sanditon, a complete enthusiast. Sanditon, the success of Sanditon as a small, fashionable bathing place, was the object for which he seemed to live. A very few years ago, it had been a quiet village of no pretensions, but some natural advantages in its position and some accidental circumstances having suggested to himself and the other principal landholder the probability of its becoming a profitable speculation, they had engaged in it, and planned and built, and praised and puffed, and raised it to something of young renown, and Mr Parker could now think of very little besides.

The facts which, in more direct communication, he laid before them were that he was about five and thirty, had been married, very happily married, seven years, and had four sweet children at home; that he was of a respectable family and easy, though not large, fortune; no profession, succeeding as eldest son to the property which two or three generations had been holding and accumulating before him; that he had two brothers and two sisters, all single and all independent, the eldest of the two former indeed, by collateral inheritance, quite as well provided for as himself. His object in quitting the high road to hunt for an advertising surgeon was also plainly stated. It had not proceeded from any intention of spraining his ankle or doing himself any other injury for the good of such surgeon, nor (as Mr Heywood had been apt to suppose) from any design of entering into partnership with him; it was merely in consequence of a wish to establish some medical man at Sanditon, which the nature of the advertisement induced him to expect to accomplish in Willingden. He was convinced that the advantage of a medical man at hand would very materially promote the rise and prosperity of the place, would in fact tend to bring a prodigious influx; nothing else was wanting. He had strong reason to believe that one family had been deterred last year from trying Sanditon on that account, and probably very many more, and his own sisters, who were sad invalids and whom he was very anxious to get to Sanditon this summer, could hardly be expected to hazard themselves in a place where they could not have immediate medical advice.

Upon the whole, Mr Parker was evidently an amiable family man, fond of wife, children, brothers and sisters, and generally kind-hearted; liberal, gentlemanlike, easy to please; of a sanguine turn of mind, with more imagination than judgement.

And Mrs Parker was as evidently a gentle, amiable, sweet-tempered woman, the properest wife in the world for a man of strong understanding but not of a capacity to supply the cooler reflection which her own husband sometimes needed; and so entirely waiting to be guided on every occasion that whether he was risking his fortune or spraining his ankle, she remained equally useless.

Sanditon was a second wife and four children to him, hardly less dear, and certainly more engrossing. He could talk of it forever. It had indeed the highest claims – not only those of birthplace, property and home; it was his mine, his lottery, his speculation and his hobby horse; his occupation, his hope and his futurity. He was extremely desirous of drawing his good friends at Willingden thither, and his endeavours in the cause were as grateful and disinterested as they were warm. He wanted to secure the promise of a visit, to get as many of the family as his own house would contain to follow him to Sanditon as soon as possible; and, healthy as they all undeniably were, foresaw that every one of them would be benefited by the sea. He held it indeed as certain that no person could be really well, no person (however upheld for the present by fortuitous aids of exercise and spirits in a semblance of health) could be really in a state of secure and permanent health without spending at least six weeks by the sea every year. The sea air and sea bathing together were nearly infallible, one or the other of them being a match for every disorder of the stomach, the lungs or the blood. They were anti-spasmodic, anti-pulmonary, anti-septic, anti-bilious and anti-rheumatic. Nobody could catch cold by the sea, nobody wanted appetite by the sea, nobody wanted spirits, nobody wanted strength. They were healing, softening, relaxing, fortifying and bracing, seemingly just as was wanted, sometimes one, sometimes the other. If the sea breeze failed, the sea bath was the certain corrective; and where bathing disagreed, the sea air alone was evidently designed by nature for the cure.

His eloquence, however, could not prevail. Mr and Mrs Heywood never left home. Marrying early and having a very numerous family, their movements had long been limited to one small circle, and they were older in habits than in age. Excepting two journeys to London in the year to receive his dividends, Mr Heywood went no farther than his feet or his well-tried old horse could carry him, and Mrs Heywood's adventures were only now and then to visit her neighbours in the old coach which had been new when they married and fresh lined on their eldest son's coming of age ten years ago. They had a very pretty property; enough, had their family been of reasonable limits, to have allowed them a very gentlemanlike share of luxuries and change; enough for them to have indulged in a new carriage and better roads, an occasional month at Tunbridge Wells, and symptoms of the gout and a winter at Bath. But the maintenance, education and fitting out of fourteen children demanded a very quiet, settled, careful course of life, and obliged them to be stationary and healthy at Willingden. What prudence had at first enjoined was now rendered pleasant by habit. They never left home and they had gratification in saying so.

But very far from wishing their children to do the same, they were glad to promote their getting out into the world as much as possible. They stayed at home that their children might get out; and, while making that home extremely comfortable, welcomed every change from it which could give useful connections or respectable acquaintance to sons or daughters. When Mr and Mrs Parker, therefore, ceased from soliciting a family visit and bounded their views to carrying back one daughter with them, no difficulties were started. It was general pleasure and consent. Their invitation was to Miss Charlotte Heywood, a very pleasing young woman of two and twenty, the eldest of the daughters at home and the one who, under her mother's directions, had been particularly useful and obliging to them; who had attended them most and knew them best. Charlotte was to go, with excellent health, to bathe and be better if she could; to receive every possible pleasure which Sanditon could be made to supply by the gratitude of those she went with; and to buy new parasols, new gloves and new brooches for her sisters and herself at the library, which Mr Parker was anxiously wishing to support. All that Mr Heywood himself could be persuaded to promise was that he would send everyone to Sanditon who asked his advice, and that nothing should ever induce him (as far as the future could be answered for) to spend even five shilling at Brinshore.

CHAPTER THREE

Every neighbourhood should have a great lady. The great lady of Sanditon was Lady Denham, and in their journey from Willingden to the coast, Mr Parker gave Charlotte a more detailed account of her than had been called for before. She had been necessarily often mentioned at Willingden, for being his colleague in speculation, Sanditon itself could not be talked of long without the introduction of Lady Denham. That she was a very rich old lady, who had buried two husbands, who knew the value of money, was very much looked up to and had a poor cousin living with her, were facts already well known; but some further particulars of her history and her character served to lighten the tediousness of a long hill, or a heavy bit of road, and to give the visiting young lady a suitable knowledge of the person with whom she might now expect to be daily associating.

Lady Denham had been a rich Miss Brereton, born to wealth but not to education. Her first husband had been a Mr Hollis, a man of considerable property in the country, of which a large share of the parish of Sanditon, with manor and mansion house, made a part. He had been an elderly man when she married him, her own age about thirty. Her motives for such a match could be little understood at the distance of forty years, but she had so well nursed and pleased Mr Hollis that at his death he left her everything – all his estates, and all at her disposal. After a widowhood of some years, she had been induced to marry again. The late Sir Harry Denham, of Denham Park in the neighbourhood of Sanditon, had succeeded in removing her and her large income to his own domains, but he could not succeed in the views of permanently enriching his family, which were attributed to him. She had been too wary to put anything out of her own power and when, on Sir Harry's decease, she returned again to her own house at Sanditon, she was said to have made this boast to a friend: 'that though she had got nothing but her title from the family, still she had given nothing for it'. For the title it was to be supposed that she had married, and Mr Parker acknowledged there being just such a degree of value for it apparent now as to give her conduct that natural explanation.

'There is at times,' said he, 'a little self-importance, but it is not offensive. And there are moments, there are points, when her love of money is carried greatly too far. But she is a good-natured woman, a very good-natured woman; a very obliging, friendly neighbour; a cheerful, independent, valuable character, and her faults may be entirely imputed to her want of education. She has good natural sense, but quite uncultivated. She has a fine active mind as well as a fine healthy frame for a woman of seventy, and enters into the improvement of Sanditon with a spirit truly admirable, though now and then, a littleness will appear. She cannot look forward quite as I would have her, and takes alarm at a trifling present expense without considering what returns it will make her in a year or two. That is, we think differently, we now and then see things differently, Miss Heywood. Those who tell their own story, you know, must be listened to with caution. When you see us in contact, you will judge for yourself.'

Lady Denham was indeed a great lady beyond the common wants of society, for she had many thousands a year to bequeath, and three distinct sets of people to be courted by: her own relations, who might very reasonably wish for her original thirty thousand pounds among them; the legal heirs of Mr Hollis, who must hope to be more indebted to her sense of justice than he had allowed them to be to his; and those members of the Denham family whom her second husband had hoped to make a good bargain for. By all of these, or by branches of them, she had no doubt been long, and still continued to be, well attacked; and of these three divisions, Mr Parker did not hesitate to say that Mr Hollis' kindred were the least in favour and Sir Harry Denham's the most. The former, he believed, had done themselves irremediable harm by expressions of very unwise and unjustifiable resentment at the time of Mr Hollis' death; the latter, to the advantage of being the remnant of a connection which she certainly valued, joined those of having been known to her from their childhood, and of being always at hand to preserve their interest by reasonable attention.

Sir Edward, the present baronet, nephew to Sir Harry, resided constantly at Denham Park, and Mr Parker had little doubt that he and his sister, Miss Denham, who lived with him, would be principally remembered in her will. He sincerely hoped it. Miss Denham had a very small provision, and her brother was a poor man for his rank in society. 'He is a warm friend to Sanditon,' said Mr Parker, 'and his hand would be as liberal as his heart, had he the power. He would be a noble coadjutor! As it is, he does what he can, and is running up a tasteful little Cottage Ornée[1] on a strip of waste ground Lady Denham has granted him, which I have no doubt we shall have many a candidate for before the end even of this season.'

Until within the last twelvemonth, Mr Parker had considered Sir Edward as standing without a rival, as having the fairest chance of succeeding to the greater part of all that she had to give; but there were now another person's claims to be taken into account, those of the young female relation whom Lady Denham had been induced to receive into her family. After having always protested against any such addition, and long and often enjoyed the repeated defeats she had given to every attempt of her relations to introduce this young lady or that young lady as a companion at Sanditon House, she had brought back with her from London last Michaelmas a Miss Brereton, who bid fair by her merits to vie in favour with Sir Edward and to secure for herself and her family that share of the accumulated property which they had certainly the best right to inherit.

Mr Parker spoke warmly of Clara Brereton, and the interest of his story increased very much with the introduction of such a character. Charlotte listened with more than amusement now; it was solicitude and enjoyment, as she heard her described to be lovely, amiable, gentle, unassuming, conducting herself uniformly with great good sense, and evidently gaining by her innate worth on the affections of her patroness. Beauty, sweetness, poverty and dependence do not want the imagination of a man to operate upon; with due exceptions, woman feels for woman very promptly and compassionately. He gave the particulars which had led to Clara's admission at Sanditon as no bad exemplification of that mixture of character, that union of littleness with kindness and good sense, with even liberality, which he saw in Lady Denham.

After having avoided London for many years, principally on account of these very cousins who were continually writing, inviting and tormenting her, and whom she was determined to keep at a distance, she had been obliged to go there last Michaelmas with the certainty of being detained at least a fortnight. She had gone to a hotel, living by her own account as prudently as possible to defy the reputed expensiveness of such a home, and at the end of three days calling for her bill that she might judge of her state. Its amount was such as determined her on staying not another hour in the house, and she was preparing, in all the anger and perturbation of a belief in very gross imposition there, and ignorance of where to go for better usage, to leave the hotel at all hazards, when the cousins, the politic and lucky cousins, who seemed always to have a spy on her, introduced themselves at this important moment; and learning her situation, persuaded her to accept such a home for the rest of her stay as their humbler house in a very inferior part of London could offer. She went, was delighted with her welcome and the hospitality and attention she received from everybody, found her good cousins the Breretons beyond her expectation worthy people, and finally was impelled by a personal knowledge of their narrow income and pecuniary difficulties to invite one of the girls of the family to pass the winter with her.

The invitation was to one, for six months, with the probability of another being then to take her place; but in selecting the one, Lady Denham had shown the good part of her character. For, passing by the actual daughters of the house, she had chosen Clara, a niece, more helpless and more pitiable of course than any, a dependent on poverty, an additional burden on an encumbered circle; and one who had been so low in every worldly view as, with all her natural endowments and powers, to have been preparing for a situation little better than a nursery maid. Clara had returned with her, and by her good sense and merit had now, to all appearance, secured a very strong hold in Lady Denham's regard. The six months had long been over and not a syllable was breathed of any change or exchange. She was a general favourite. The influence of her steady conduct and mild, gentle temper was felt by everybody. The prejudices which had met her at first, in some quarters, were all dissipated. She was felt to be worthy of trust, to be the very companion who would guide and soften Lady Denham, who would enlarge her mind and open her hand. She was as thoroughly amiable as she was lovely; and since having had the advantage of their Sanditon breezes, that loveliness was complete.

CHAPTER FOUR

'And whose very snug-looking place is this?' said Charlotte as, in a sheltered dip within two miles of the sea, they passed close by a moderate-sized house, well fenced and planted, and rich in the garden, orchard and meadows, which are the best embellishments of such a dwelling. 'It seems to have as many comforts about it as Willingden.'

'Ah,' said Mr Parker. 'This is my old house, the house of my forefathers, the house where I and all my brothers and sisters were born and bred, and where my own three eldest children were born; where Mrs Parker and I lived until within the last two years, when our new house was finished. I am glad you are pleased with it. It is an honest old place, and Hillier keeps it in very good order. I have given it up, you know, to the man who occupies the chief of my land. He gets a better house by it, and I, a rather better situation!

'One other hill brings us to Sanditon, modern Sanditon, a beautiful spot. Our ancestors, you know, always built in a hole, Here were we, pent down in this little contracted nook, without air or view, only one mile and three quarters from the noblest expanse of ocean between the south foreland and the land's end, and without the smallest advantage from it. You will not think I have made a bad exchange when we reach Trafalgar House, which by the by, I almost wish I had not named Trafalgar, for Waterloo is more the thing now. However, Waterloo is in reserve, and if we have encouragement enough this year for a little crescent to be ventured on (as I trust we shall) then we shall be able to call it Waterloo Crescent, and the name joined to the form of the building, which always takes, will give us the command of lodgers. In a good season we should have more applications than we could attend to.'

'It was always a very comfortable house,' said Mrs Parker, looking at it through the back window with something like the fondness of regret. 'And such a nice garden, such an excellent garden.'

'Yes, my love, but that we may be said to carry with us. It supplies us, as before, with all the fruit and vegetables we want, and we have, in fact, all the comfort of an excellent kitchen garden without the constant eyesore of its formalities or the yearly nuisance of its decaying vegetation. Who can endure a cabbage bed in October?'

'Oh! Dear, yes. We are quite as well off for garden stuff as ever we were, for if it is forgot to be brought at any time, we can always buy what we want at Sanditon House. The gardener there is glad enough to supply us. But it was a nice place for the children to run about in. So shady in summer!'

'My dear, we shall have shade enough on the hill, and more than enough in the course of a very few years. The growth of my plantations is a general astonishment. In the meanwhile we have the canvas awning, which gives us the most complete comfort within doors, and you can get a parasol at Whitby's for little Mary at any time, or a large bonnet at Jebb's. And as for the boys, I must say I would rather them run about in the sunshine than not. I am sure we agree, my dear, in wishing our boys to be as hardy as possible.'

'Yes indeed, I am sure we do. And I will get Mary a little parasol, which will make her as proud as can be. How grave she will walk about with it, and fancy herself quite a little woman. Oh! I have not the smallest doubt of our being a great deal better off where we are now. If we any of us want to bathe, we have not a quarter of a mile to go. But you know,' – still looking back – 'one loves to look at an old friend, at a place where one has been happy. The Hilliers did not seem to feel the storms last winter at all. I remember seeing Mrs Hillier after one of those dreadful nights, when we had been literally rocked in our bed, and she did not seem at all aware of the wind being anything more than common.'

'Yes, yes, that's likely enough. We have all the grandeur of the storm with less real danger because the wind, meeting with nothing to oppose or confine it around our house, simply rages and passes on; while down in this gutter, nothing is known of the state of the air below the tops of the trees; and the inhabitants may be taken totally unawares by one of those dreadful currents, which do more mischief in a valley when they do arise than an open country ever experiences in the heaviest gale. But, my dear love, as to garden stuff, you were saying that any accidental omission is supplied in a moment by Lady Denham's gardener, but it occurs to me that we ought to go elsewhere upon such occasions, and that old Stringer and his son have a higher claim. I encouraged him to set up, and am afraid he does not do very well – that is, there has not been time enough yet. He will do very well beyond a doubt, but at first it is uphill work, and therefore we must give him what help we can, and when any vegetables or fruit happen to be wanted – and it will not be amiss to have them often wanted, to have something or other forgotten most days – just to have a nominal supply, you know, that poor old Andrew may not lose his daily job, but in fact to buy the chief of our consumption from the Stringers.'

'Very well, my love, that can be easily done, and cook will be satisfied, which will be a great comfort, for she is always complaining of old Andrew now and says he never brings her what she wants. There, now the old house is quite left behind. What is it your brother Sidney says about its being a hospital?'

'Oh! My dear Mary, merely a joke of his. He pretends to advise me to make a hospital of it. He pretends to laugh at my improvements. Sidney says anything, you know. He has always said what he chose, of and to us all. Most families have such a member among them, I believe, Miss Heywood. There is someone in most families privileged by superior abilities or spirits to say anything. In ours, it is Sidney, who is a very clever young man and with great powers of pleasing. He lives too much in the world to be settled; that is his only fault. He is here and there and everywhere. I wish we may get him to Sanditon. I should like to have you acquainted with him. And it would be a fine thing for the place! Such a young man as Sidney, with his neat equipage and fashionable air. You and I, Mary, know what effect it might have. Many a respectable family, many a careful mother, many a pretty daughter might it secure us to the prejudice of Eastbourne and Hastings.'

They were now approaching the church and real village of Sanditon, which stood at the foot of the hill they were afterwards to ascend, a hill whose side was covered with the woods and enclosures of Sanditon House and whose height ended in an open down where the new buildings might soon be looked for. A branch only of the valley, winding more obliquely towards the sea, gave a passage to an inconsiderable stream, and formed at its mouth a third habitable division in a small cluster of fishermen's houses. The village contained little more than cottages, but the spirit of the day had been caught, as Mr Parker observed with delight to Charlotte, and two or three of the best of them were smartened up with a white curtain and 'Lodgings to let'; and farther on, in the little green court of an old farmhouse, two females in elegant white were actually to be seen with their books and camp stools; and in turning the corner of the baker's shop, the sound of a harp might be heard through the upper casement.

Such sights and sounds were highly blissful to Mr Parker. Not that he had any personal concern in the success of the village itself, for considering it as too remote from the beach, he had done nothing there; but it was a most valuable proof of the increasing fashion of the place altogether. If the *village* could attract, the hill might be nearly full. He anticipated an amazing season. At the same time last year (late in July) there had not been a single lodger in the village! Nor did he remember any during the whole summer, excepting one family of children who came from London for sea air after the whooping cough, and whose mother would not let them be nearer the shore for fear of their tumbling in.

'Civilisation, civilisation indeed!' cried Mr Parker, delighted. 'Look, my dear Mary, look at William Heeley's windows. Blue shoes, and nankin boots! Who would have expected such a sight at a shoemaker's in old Sanditon! This is new within the month. There was no blue shoe when we passed this way a month ago. Glorious indeed! Well, I think I have done something in my day. Now, for our hill, our health-breathing hill.'

In ascending, they passed the lodge gates of Sanditon House and saw the top of the house itself among its groves. It was the last building of former days in that line of the parish. A little higher up, the modern began; and in crossing the down, a Prospect House, a Bellevue Cottage and a Denham Place were to be looked at by Charlotte with the calmness of amused curiosity, and by Mr Parker with the eager eye which hoped to see scarcely any empty houses. More bills at the windows than he had calculated on, and a smaller show of company on the hill; fewer carriages, fewer walkers. He had fancied it just the time of day for them to be all returning from their airings to dinner; but the sands and the terrace always attracted some, and the tide must be flowing, about half-tide now. He longed to be on the sands, the cliffs, at his own house, and everywhere out of his house at once. His spirits rose with the very sight of the sea and he could almost feel his ankle getting stronger already.

Trafalgar House, on the most elevated spot on the down, was a light, elegant building, standing in a small lawn with a very young plantation round it, about a hundred yards from the brow of a steep but not very lofty cliff, and the nearest to it of every building, excepting one short row of smart-looking houses called the terrace, with a broad walk in front, aspiring to be the mall of the place. In this row were the best milliner's shop and the library; a little detached from it, the hotel and billiard room. Here began the descent to the beach and to the bathing machines, and this was therefore the favourite spot for beauty and fashion. At Trafalgar House, rising at a little distance behind the terrace, the travellers were safely set down, and all was happiness and joy between Papa and Mama and their children; while Charlotte, having received possession of her apartment, found amusement enough in standing at her ample Venetian window and looking over the miscellaneous foreground of unfinished buildings, waving linen and tops of houses, to the sea, dancing and sparkling in sunshine and freshness.

CHAPTER FIVE

When they met before dinner, Mr Parker was looking over letters. 'Not a line from Sidney!' said he. 'He is an idle fellow. I sent him an account of my accident from Willingden and thought he would have vouchsafed me an answer. But perhaps it implies that he is coming himself. I trust it may. But here is a letter from one of my sisters. *They* never fail me. Women are the only correspondents to be depended on. Now, Mary,' smiling at his wife, 'before I open it, what shall we guess as to the state of health of those it comes from, or rather what would Sidney say if he were here? Sidney is a saucy fellow, Miss Heywood. And you must know, he will have it there is a good deal of imagination in my two sisters' complaints. But it really is not so, or very little. They have wretched health, as you have heard us say frequently, and are subject to a variety of very serious disorders. Indeed, I do not believe they know what a day's health is. And at the same time, they are such excellent useful women and have so much energy of character that where any good is to be done, they force themselves on exertions which, to those who do not thoroughly know them, have an extraordinary appearance. But there is really no affectation about them, you know. They have only weaker constitutions and stronger minds than are often met with, either separate or together.

'And our youngest brother, who lives with them and who is not much above twenty, I am sorry to say is almost as great an invalid as themselves. He is so delicate that he can engage in no profession. Sidney laughs at him, but it really is no joke, though Sidney often makes me laugh at them all in spite of myself. Now, if he were here, I know he would be offering odds that either Susan, Diana or Arthur would appear by this letter to have been at the point of death within the last month.' Having run his eye over the letter, he shook his head and began, 'No chance of seeing them at Sanditon, I am sorry to say. A very indifferent account of them indeed. Seriously, a very indifferent account. Mary, you will be quite sorry to hear how ill they have been and are. Miss Heywood, if you will give me leave, I will read Diana's letter aloud. I like to have my friends acquainted with each other and I am afraid this is the only sort of acquaintance I shall have the means of accomplishing between you. And I can have no scruple on Diana's account, for her letters show her exactly as she is, the most active, friendly, warm-hearted being in existence, and therefore must give a good impression.' He read:

'My dear Tom, we were all much grieved at your accident, and if you had not described yourself as fallen into such very good hands, I should have been with you at all hazards the day after the receipt of your letter, though it found me suffering under a more severe attack than usual of my old grievance, spasmodic bile, and hardly able to crawl from my bed to the sofa. But how were you treated? Send me more particulars in your next. If indeed a simple sprain, as you denominate it, nothing would have been so judicious as friction, friction by the hand alone, supposing it could be applied instantly. Two years ago I happened to be calling on Mrs Sheldon when her coachman sprained his foot as he was cleaning the carriage and could hardly limp into the house, but by the immediate use of friction alone, steadily persevered in (and I rubbed his ankle with my own hand for six hours without intermission), he was well in three days.

'Many thanks, my dear Tom, for the kindness with respect to us, which had so large a share in bringing on *your accident. But pray never run into peril again in looking for an apothecary on our account, for had you the most experienced man in his line settled at Sanditon, it would be no recommendation to us. We have entirely done with the whole medical tribe. We have consulted physician after physician in vain, until we are quite convinced that they can do nothing for us and that we must trust to our own knowledge of our own wretched constitutions for any relief. But if you think it advisable for the interest of the place to get a medical man there, I will undertake the commission with pleasure, and have no doubt of succeeding. I could soon put the necessary irons in the fire. As for getting to Sanditon myself, it is quite an impossibility. I grieve to say that I dare not attempt it, but my feelings tell me too plainly that, in my present state, the sea air would probably be the death of me. And neither of my dear companions will leave me or I would promote their going down to you for a fortnight. But in truth, I doubt whether Susan's nerves would be equal to the effort. She has been suffering much from the headache, and six leeches a day for ten days together relieved her so little that we thought it right to change our measures, and being convinced on examination that much of the evil lay in her gum, I persuaded her to attack the disorder there. She has accordingly had three teeth drawn, and is decidedly better, but her nerves are a good deal deranged. She can only speak in a whisper and fainted away twice this morning on poor Arthur's trying to suppress a cough.*

'He, I am happy to say, is tolerably well, though more languid than I like, and I fear for his liver. I have heard nothing of Sidney since your being together in town, but conclude his scheme to the Isle of Wight has not taken

place or we should have seen him in his way. Most sincerely do we wish you a good season at Sanditon, and though we cannot contribute to your beau monde *in person, we are doing our utmost to send you company worth having and think we may safely reckon on securing you two large families. One a rich West Indian from Surrey, the other a most respectable Girls' Boarding School, or Academy, from Camberwell. I will not tell you how many people I have employed in the business, wheel within wheel, but success more than repays. Yours most affectionately, etcetera.*

'Well,' said Mr Parker, as he finished. 'Though I dare say Sidney might find something extremely entertaining in this letter and make us laugh for half an hour together, I declare I by myself can see nothing in it but what is either very pitiable or very creditable. With all their sufferings, you perceive how much they are occupied in promoting the good of others! So anxious for Sanditon! Two large families, one for Prospect House probably, the other for number two Denham Place or the end house of the terrace, and extra beds at the hotel. I told you my sisters were excellent women, Miss Heywood.'

'And I am sure they must be very extraordinary ones,' said Charlotte. 'I am astonished at the cheerful style of the letter, considering the state in which both sisters appear to be. Three teeth drawn at once. Frightful! Your sister Diana seems almost as ill as possible, but those three teeth of your sister Susan are more distressing than all the rest.'

'Oh! They are so used to the operation, to every operation, and have such fortitude!'

'Your sisters know what they are about, I dare say, but their measures seem to touch on extremes. I feel that, in any illness,

I should be so anxious for professional advice, so very little venturesome for myself or anybody I loved! But then, *we* have been so healthy a family that I can be no judge of what the habit of self-doctoring may do.'

'Why, to own the truth,' said Mrs Parker, 'I do think the Miss Parkers carry it too far sometimes. And so do you, my love, you know. You often think they would be better if they would leave themselves more alone, and especially Arthur. I know you think it a great pity they should give him such a turn for being ill.'

'Well, well, my dear Mary, I grant you, it is unfortunate for poor Arthur that at his time of life he should be encouraged to give way to indisposition. It is bad – it is bad that he should be fancying himself too sickly for any profession, and sit down at one and twenty, on the interest of his own little fortune, without any idea of attempting to improve it, or of engaging in any occupation that may be of use to himself or others. But let us talk of pleasanter things. These two large families are just what we wanted. But here is something at hand pleasanter still, Morgan with his "Dinner on table".'

The party were very soon moving after dinner. Mr Parker could not be satisfied without an early visit to the library, and the library subscription book, and Charlotte was glad to see as much, and as quickly as possible, where all was new. They were out in the very quietest part of a wateringplace day, when the important business of dinner or of sitting after dinner was going on in almost every inhabited lodging. Here and there a solitary elderly man might be seen, who was forced to move early and walk for health, but in general, it was a thorough pause of company, it was the emptiness and tranquillity on the terrace, the cliffs and the sands. The shops were deserted, the straw hats and pendant lace seemed left to their fate both within the house and without, and Mrs Whitby at the library was sitting in her inner room, reading one of her own novels for want of employment.

The list of subscribers was but commonplace. The Lady Denham, Miss Brereton, Mr and Mrs Parker, Sir Edward Denham and Miss Denham, whose names might be said to lead off the season, were followed by nothing better than Mrs Matthews, Miss Matthews, Miss E. Matthews, Miss H. Matthews; Dr and Mrs Brown; Mr Richard Pratt; Lieut. Smith R.N. Capt.; Little, Limehouse; Mrs Jane Fisher; Miss Scroggs; Revd Mr Hanking; Mr Beard, solicitor, Gray's Inn; Mrs Davis and Miss Merryweather. Mr Parker could not but feel that the list was not only without distinction, but less numerous than he had hoped.

It was but July however, and August and September were the months. And besides, the promised large families from Surrey and Camberwell were an ever-ready consolation. Mrs Whitby came forward without delay from her literary recess, delighted to see Mr Parker again, whose manners recommended him to everybody. They were fully occupied in their various civilities and communications, while Charlotte, having added her name to the list as the first offering to the success of the season, was busy in some immediate purchases for the further good of everybody as soon as Miss Whitby could be hurried down from her toilette, with all her glossy curls and smart trinkets to wait on her.

The library, of course, afforded everything, all the useless things in the world that could not be done without, and among so many pretty temptations, and with so much good will for Mr Parker to encourage expenditure, Charlotte began to feel that she must check herself, or rather she reflected that at two and twenty there could be no excuse for her doing otherwise, and that it would not do for her to be spending all her money the very first evening. She took up a book; it happened to be a volume of *Camilla*.[2] She had not Camilla's youth, and had no intention of having her distress, so she turned from the drawers of rings and brooches, repressed farther solicitation, and paid for what she bought.

For her particular gratification, they were then to take a turn on the cliff, but as they quitted the library they were met by two ladies whose arrival made an alteration necessary: Lady Denham and Miss Brereton. They had been to Trafalgar House, and had been directed hence to the library. Though Lady Denham was a great deal too active to regard the walk of a mile as anything requiring rest, and talked of going home again directly, the Parkers knew that to be pressed into their house and obliged to take her tea with them would suit her best, and therefore a stroll on the cliff gave way to an immediate return home.

'No, no,' said her Ladyship, 'I will not have you hurry your tea on my account. I know you like your tea late. My early hours are not to put my neighbours to inconvenience. No, no, Miss Clara and I will get back to our own tea. We came out with no other thought. We just wanted to see you and make sure of your being really come, but we get back to our own tea.'

She went on however towards Trafalgar House and took possession of the drawing room very quietly, without seeming to hear a word of Mrs Parker's orders to the servant as they entered to bring tea directly. Charlotte was fully consoled for the loss of her walk by finding herself in company of those whom the conversation of the morning had given her a great curiosity to see. She observed them well.

Lady Denham was of middle height, stout, upright and alert in her motions, with a shrewd eye and self-satisfied air, but not an unagreeable countenance. Though her manner was rather downright and abrupt as of a person who valued herself on being free-spoken, there was a good humour and cordiality about her, a civility and readiness to be acquainted with Charlotte herself, and a heartiness of welcome towards her old friends, which was inspiring the good will she seemed to feel.

And as for Miss Brereton, her appearance so completely justified Mr Parker's praise that Charlotte thought she had never beheld a more lovely or more interesting young woman. Elegantly tall, regularly handsome, with great delicacy of complexion and soft blue eyes, a sweetly modest and yet naturally graceful address, Charlotte could see in her only the most perfect representation of whatever heroine might be most beautiful and bewitching in all the numerous volumes they had left behind them on Mrs Whitby's shelves. Perhaps it might be partly owing to her having just issued from a circulating library, but she could not separate the idea of a complete heroine from Clara Brereton. Her situation with Lady Denham so very much in favour of it! She seemed placed with her on purpose to be ill-used. Such poverty and dependence joined to such beauty and merit seemed to leave no choice in the business.

These feelings were not the result of any romance in Charlotte herself. No, she was a very sober-minded young lady, sufficiently well read in novels to supply her imagination with amusement, but not at all unreasonably influenced by them. While she pleased herself the first five minutes with fancying the persecutions which ought to be the lot of the interesting Clara, especially in the form of the most barbarous conduct on Lady Denham's side, she found no reluctance to admit from subsequent observation that they appeared to be on very comfortable terms. She could see nothing worse in Lady Denham, than the sort of old-fashioned formality of always calling her 'Miss Clara', nor anything objectionable in the degree of observance and attention which Clara paid. On one side it seemed protecting kindness, on the other grateful and affectionate respect.

The conversation turned entirely upon Sanditon, its present number of visitants and the chances of a good season. t was evident that Lady Denham had more anxiety, more fears of loss, than her coadjutor. She wanted to have the place fill faster, and seemed to have many harassing apprehensions of the lodgings being in some instances underlet. Miss Diana Parker's two large families were not forgotten.

'Very good, very good,' said her Ladyship. 'A West Indian family and a school. That sounds well. That will bring money.'

'No people spend more freely, I believe, than West Indians,' observed Mr Parker.

'Aye, so I have heard, and because they have full purses, fancy themselves equal, maybe, to your old country families. But then, they who scatter their money so freely never think of whether they may not be doing mischief by raising the price of things. And I have heard that's very much the case with your West Indians, and if they come among us to raise the price of our necessaries in life, we shall not much thank them, Mr Parker.'

'My dear Madam, they can only raise the price of consumable articles, by such an extraordinary demand for them and such a diffusion of money among us, as must do us more good than harm. Our butchers and bakers and traders in general cannot get rich without bringing prosperity to us. If *they* do not gain, our rents must be insecure, and in proportion to their profit must be ours eventually in the increased value of our houses.'

'Oh! Well. But I should not like to have butcher's meat raised, though, and I shall keep it down as long as I can. Aye, that young lady smiles I see, I dare say she thinks me an odd sort of creature, but she will come to care about such matters herself in time. Yes, yes, my dear, depend upon it, you will be thinking of the price of butcher's meat in time, though you may not happen to have quite such a servants' hall full to feed, as I have. And I do not believe those are the best off that have fewest servants. I am not a woman of parade, as all the world knows, and if it was not for what I owe to poor Mr Hollis' memory, I should never keep up Sanditon House as I do; it is not from my own pleasure.

'Well Mr Parker, and the other is a boarding school, a French boarding school, is it? No harm in that. They'll stay their six weeks. And out of such a number, who knows but some may be consumptive and want asses' milk, and I have two milch asses at this present time. But perhaps the little Misses may hurt the furniture. I hope they will have a good sharp governess to look after them.'

Poor Mr Parker got no more credit from Lady Denham than he had from his sisters, for the object which had taken him to Willingden. 'Lord! My dear sir,' she cried, 'how could you think of such a thing? I am very sorry you met with your accident, but upon my word you deserved it. Going after a doctor! Why, what should we do with a doctor here? It would be only encouraging our servants and the poor to fancy themselves ill, if there was a doctor at hand. Oh! Pray, let us have none of the tribe at Sanditon. We go on very well as we are. There is the sea and the downs and my milch asses, and I have told Mrs Whitby that if anybody enquires for a chamber-horse, they may be supplied at a fair rate (poor Mr Hollis' chamber-horse, as good as new) and what can people want for more? Here have I lived seventy good years in the world and never took physic above twice, and never saw the face of a doctor in all my life, on my own account. And I verily believe if my poor dead Sir Harry had never seen one neither, he would have been alive now. Ten fees, one after another, did the man take who sent him out of the world. I beseech you Mr Parker, no doctors here.'

The tea things were brought in. 'Oh! My dear Mrs Parker, you should not indeed, why would you do so? I was just upon the point of wishing you good evening. But since you are so neighbourly, I believe Miss Clara and I must stay.'

The popularity of the Parkers brought them some visitors the very next morning, amongst them, Sir Edward Denham and his sister, who having been at Sanditon House drove on to pay their compliments. The duty of letter-writing being accomplished, Charlotte was settled with Mrs Parker in the drawing room in time to see them all.

The Denhams were the only ones to excite particular attention. Charlotte was glad to complete her knowledge of the family by an introduction to them, and found them, the better half at least (for while single, the gentleman may sometimes be thought the better half of the pair) not unworthy of notice. Miss Denham was a fine young woman, but cold and reserved, giving the idea of one who felt her consequence with pride and her poverty with discontent, and who was immediately gnawed by want of a handsomer equipage than the simple gig in which they travelled, and which their groom was leading about still in her sight. Sir Edward was much her superior in air and manner, certainly handsome, but yet more to be remarked for his very good address and wish of paying attention and giving pleasure. He came into the room remarkably well, talked much – and very much to Charlotte, by whom he chanced to be placed – and she soon perceived that he had a fine countenance, a most pleasing gentleness of voice and a great deal of conversation. She liked him. Sober-minded as she was, she thought him agreeable and did not quarrel with the suspicion of his finding her equally so, which would arise from his evidently disregarding his sister's motion to go, and persisting in his station and his discourse.

I make no apologies for my heroine's vanity. If there are young ladies in the world at her time of life, more dull of fancy and more careless of pleasing, I know them not, and never wish to know them.

At last, from the low French windows of the drawing room which commanded the road and all the paths across the down, Charlotte and Sir Edward as they sat could not but observe Lady Denham and Miss Brereton walking by, and there was instantly a slight change in Sir Edward's countenance, with an anxious glance after them as they proceeded followed by an anxious proposal to his sister, not merely for moving, but for walking on together to the terrace, which altogether gave a hasty turn to Charlotte's fancy, cured her of her half hour's fever, and placed her in a more capable state of judging, when Sir Edward was gone, of how agreeable he had actually been. 'Perhaps there was a good deal of air and address, and his title did him no harm.'

She was very soon in his company again. The first object of the Parkers, when their house was cleared of morning visitors, was to get out themselves; the terrace was the attraction to all. Everybody who walked must begin with the terrace, and there, seated on one of the two green benches by the gravel walk, they found the Denham party; but though united in the gross, very distinctly divided again, the two superior Ladies being at one end of the bench, and Sir Edward and Miss Brereton at the other. Charlotte's first glance told her that Sir Edward's air was that of a lover. There could be no doubt of his devotion to Clara. How Clara received it was less obvious, but she was inclined to think not very favourably, for though sitting thus apart with him (which probably she might not have been able to prevent), her air was calm and grave. That the young lady at the other end of the bench was doing penance was indubitable. The difference in Miss Denham's countenance, the change from Miss Denham sitting in cold grandeur in Mrs

Parker's drawing room to be kept from silence by the efforts of others, to Miss Denham at Lady Denham's elbow, listening and talking with smiling attention or solicitous eagerness, was very striking, and very amusing, or very melancholy, just as satire or morality might prevail.

Miss Denham's character was pretty well decided by Charlotte. Sir Edward's required longer observation. He surprised her by quitting Clara immediately on their all joining and agreeing to walk and by addressing his attentions entirely to herself. Stationing himself close by her, he seemed to mean to detach her as much as possible from the rest of the party and to give her the whole of his conversation. He began, in a tone of great taste and feeling, to talk of the sea and the seashore, and ran with energy through all the usual phrases employed in praise of their sublimity, and descriptive of the indescribable emotions they excite in the mind of sensibility. The terrific grandeur of the ocean in a storm, its glassy surface in a calm, its gulls and its samphire, and in the deep fathoms of its abysses, its quick vicissitudes, its direful deceptions, its mariners tempting it in sunshine and overwhelmed by the sudden tempest, all were eagerly and fluently touched – rather commonplace perhaps, but doing very well from the lips of a handsome Sir Edward, and she could not but think of him as a man of feeling until he began to stagger her by the number of his quotations, and the bewilderment of some of his sentences.

'Do you remember,' said he, 'Scott's beautiful lines on the sea? Oh! What a description they convey! They are never out of my thoughts when I walk here. That man who can read them unmoved must have the nerves of an assassin! Heaven defend me from meeting such a man unarmed.'

'What description do you mean?' said Charlotte. 'I remember none at this moment, of the sea, in either of Scott's poems.'

'Do you not indeed? Nor can I exactly recall the beginning at this moment. But you cannot have forgotten his description of woman:

Oh! Woman in our Hours of Ease…

'Delicious! Delicious! Had he written nothing more, he would have been immortal. And then again, that unequalled, unrivalled address to parental affection:

Some feelings are to mortals given
With less of Earth in them than Heaven.

'But while we are on the subject of poetry, what think you, Miss Heywood, of Burns' lines to his Mary? Oh! There is pathos to madden one! If ever there was a man who *felt*, it was Burns. Montgomery has all the fire of poetry, Wordsworth has the true soul of it, Campbell in his *Pleasures of Hope* has touched the extreme of our sensations, "like angels' visits, few and far between". Can you conceive of anything more subduing, more melting, more fraught with the deep sublime than that line?

'But Burns, I confess my sense of his pre-eminence, Miss Heywood. If Scott has a fault, it is the want of passion. Tender, elegant, descriptive but tame. The man who cannot do justice to the attributes of woman is my contempt. Sometimes indeed a flash of feeling seems to irradiate him, as in the lines we were speaking of, "Oh! Woman in our hours of ease". But Burns is always on fire. His soul was the altar in which lovely woman sat enshrined, his spirit truly breathed the immortal incense which is her due.'

'I have read several of Burns' poems with great delight,' said Charlotte as soon as she had time to speak, 'but I am not poetic enough to separate a man's poetry entirely from his character, and poor Burns' known irregularities greatly interrupt my enjoyment of his lines. I have difficulty in depending on the truth of his feelings as a lover. I have not faith in the sincerity of the affections of a man of his description. He felt and he wrote and he forgot.'

'Oh! No, no,' exclaimed Sir Edward in an ecstasy. 'He was all ardour and truth! His genius and his susceptibilities might lead him into some aberrations. But who is perfect? It were hyper-criticism, it were pseudo-philosophy to expect from the soul of high-toned genius, the grovellings of a common mind. The coruscations of talent, elicited by impassioned feeling in the breast of man, are perhaps incompatible with some of the prosaic decencies of life; nor can you, loveliest Miss Heywood (speaking with an air of deep sentiment), nor can any woman be a fair judge of what a man may be propelled to say, write or do, by the sovereign impulses of illimitable ardour.'

This was very fine, but if Charlotte understood it at all, not very moral, and being moreover by no means pleased with his extraordinary style of compliment, she gravely answered, 'I really know nothing of the matter. This is a charming day. The wind I fancy must be southerly.'

'Happy, happy wind, to engage Miss Heywood's thoughts!' She began to think him downright silly. His choosing to walk with her, she had learnt to understand. It was done to pique Miss Brereton. She had read it, in an anxious glance or two on his side, but why he should talk so much nonsense, unless he could do no better, was unintelligible. He seemed very sentimental, very full of some feelings or other, and very much addicted to all the newest-fashioned hard words; had not a very clear brain, she presumed, and talked a good deal by rote. The future might explain him further, but when there was a proposition for going into the library she felt that she had had quite enough of Sir Edward for one morning, and very gladly accepted Lady Denham's invitation of remaining on the terrace with her.

The others all left them, Sir Edward with looks of very gallant despair in tearing himself away, and they united their agreeableness – that is, Lady Denham, like a true great lady, talked and talked only of her own concerns, and Charlotte listened, amused in considering the contrast between her two companions. Certainly, there was no strain of doubtful sentiment, nor any phrase of difficult interpretation in Lady Denham's discourse. Taking hold of Charlotte's arm with the ease of one who felt that any notice from her was an honour, and communicative, from the influence of the same conscious importance or natural love of talking, she immediately said in a tone of great satisfaction and with a look of arch sagacity, 'Miss Esther wants me to invite her and her brother to spend a week with me at Sanditon House, as I did last summer, but I shan't. She has been trying to get round me every way, with her praise of this, and her praise of that, but I saw what she was about. I saw through it all. I am not very easily taken in, my dear.'

Charlotte could think of nothing more harmless to be said, than the simple enquiry of, 'Sir Edward and Miss Denham?'

'Yes, my dear. My young folks, as I call them sometimes, for I take them very much by the hand. I had them with me last summer about this time, for a week, from Monday to Monday, and very delighted and thankful they were. For they are very good young people, my dear. I would not have you think that I only notice them for poor dear Sir Harry's sake. No, no, they are very deserving themselves, or trust me, they would not be so much in *my* company. I am not the woman to help anybody blindfold. I always take care to know what I am about and who I have to deal with, before I stir a finger. I do not think I was ever overreached in my life, and that is a good deal for a woman to say that has been married twice. Poor dear Sir Harry (between ourselves) thought at first to have got more. But,' (with a bit of a sigh) 'he is gone, and we must not find fault with the dead. Nobody could live happier together than us, and he was a very honourable man, quite the gentleman of the ancient family. And when he died, I gave Sir Edward his gold watch.' She said this with a look at her companion which implied its right to produce a great impression, and seeing no rapturous astonishment in Charlotte's countenance, added quickly, 'He did not bequeath it to his nephew, my dear, it was no bequest. It was not in the will. He only told me, and that but once, that he should wish his nephew to have his watch, but it need not have been binding if I had not chose it.'

'Very kind indeed! Very handsome,' said Charlotte, absolutely forced to affect admiration.

'Yes, my dear, and it is not the only kind thing I have done by him. I have been a very liberal friend to Sir Edward. And poor young man, he needs it bad enough. For though I am only the dowager, my dear, and he is the heir, things do not stand between us in the way they commonly do between those two parties. Not a shilling do I receive from the Denham estate. Sir Edward has no payments to make me. He doesn't stand uppermost, believe me. It is I that help him.'

'Indeed! He is a very fine young man, particularly elegant in his address.' This was said chiefly for the sake of saying something, but Charlotte directly saw that it was laying her open to suspicion by Lady Denham's giving a shrewd glance at her and replying:

'Yes, yes, he is very well to look at, and it is to be hoped that some lady of large fortune will think so, for Sir Edward must marry for money. He and I often talk that matter over. A handsome young fellow like him will go smirking and smiling about and paying girls compliments but he knows he must marry for money. And Sir Edward is a very steady young man in the main, and has got very good notions.'

'Sir Edward Denham,' said Charlotte, 'with such personal advantages may be almost sure of getting a woman of fortune, if he chooses it.'

This glorious sentiment seemed quite to remove suspicion. 'Aye, my dear, that's very sensibly said,' cried Lady Denham. 'And if we could but get a young heiress to Sanditon! But heiresses are monstrous scarce! I do not think we have had an heiress here, or even a co-heiress since Sanditon has been a public place. Families come after families, but as far as I can learn, it is not one in a hundred of them that have any real property, landed or funded. An income perhaps, but no property. Clergymen maybe, or lawyers from town, or half-pay officers, or widows with only a jointure. And what good can such people do anybody? Except just as they take our empty houses, and (between ourselves) I think they are great fools for not staying at home. Now, if we could get a young heiress to be sent here for her health (and if she was ordered to drink asses' milk, I could supply her), and as soon as she got well, have her fall in love with Sir Edward!'

'That would be very fortunate indeed.'

'And Miss Esther must marry somebody of fortune too; she must get a rich husband. Ah! Young ladies that have no money are very much to be pitied! But,' after a short pause, 'if Miss

Esther thinks to talk me into inviting them to come and stay at Sanditon House, she will find herself much mistaken. Matters are altered with me since last summer you know. I have Miss Clara with me now, which makes a great difference.' She spoke this so seriously that Charlotte instantly saw in it the evidence of real penetration and prepared for some fuller remarks, but it was followed only by, 'I have no fancy for having my house as full as a hotel. I should not choose to have my two housemaids' time taken up all the morning in dusting out bedrooms. They have Miss Clara's room to put to rights as well as my own every day. If they had hard places, they would want higher wages.'

For objections of this nature, Charlotte was not prepared, and she found it so impossible even to affect sympathy that she could say nothing. Lady Denham soon added, with great glee, 'And besides all this my dear, and I to be filling my house to the prejudice of Sanditon? If people want to be by the sea, why don't they take the lodgings? Here are a great many empty houses, three on this very terrace, no fewer than three lodging papers staring us in the face at this very moment, numbers three, four and eight. Eight, the corner house, may be too large for them, but either of the two others are nice snug little houses, very fit for a young gentleman and his sister. And so, my dear, the next time Miss Esther begins talking about the dampness of Denham Park, and the good that bathing always does her, I shall advise them to come and take one of these lodgings for a fortnight. Don't you think that will be very fair? Charity begins at home, you know.'

Charlotte's feelings were divided between amusement and indignation, but indignation had the larger and increasing share. She kept her countenance and she kept a civil silence. She could not carry her forbearance farther, but without attempting to listen longer, and only conscious that Lady Denham was still talking on in the same way, allowed her thoughts to form themselves into such a meditation as this: 'She is thoroughly mean. I had not expected anything so bad. Mr Parker spoke too mildly of her. His judgement is evidently not to be trusted. His own good nature misleads him. He is too kind-hearted to see clearly. I must judge for myself. And their very connection prejudices him. He has persuaded her to engage in the same speculation, and because their object in that line is the same, he fancies she feels like him in others. But she is very, very mean. I can see no good in her. Poor Miss Brereton! And she makes everybody mean about her. This poor Sir Edward and his sister, how far nature meant them to be respectable I cannot tell, but they are obliged to be mean in their servility to her. Thus it is, when rich people are sordid.'

The two ladies continued walking together until they were rejoined by the others, who, as they issued from the library, were followed by a young Whitby running off with five volumes under his arm to Sir Edward's gig, and Sir Edward approaching Charlotte, said, 'You may perceive what has been our occupation. My sister wanted my counsel in the selection of some books. We have many leisure hours, and read a great deal. I am no indiscriminate novel-reader. The mere trash of the common circulating library, I hold in the highest contempt. You will never hear me advocating those puerile emanations which detail nothing but discordant principles incapable of amalgamation, or those vapid tissues of ordinary occurrences from which no useful deductions can be drawn. In vain may we put them into a literary alembic; we distil nothing which can add to science. You understand me, I am sure?'

'I am not quite certain that I do. But if you will describe the sort of novels which you *do* approve, I dare say it will give me a clearer idea.'

'Most willingly, fair questioner. The novels which I approve are such as display human nature with grandeur, such as show her in the sublimeness of intense feeling, such as exhibit the progress of strong passion from the first germ of incipient susceptibility to the utmost energies of reason half-dethroned, where we see the strong spark of woman's captivations elicit such fire in the soul of man as leads him (though at the risk of some aberration from the strict line of primitive obligations) to hazard all, dare all, achieve all, to obtain her.

'Such are the works which I peruse with great delight, and I hope I may say, with amelioration. They hold forth the most splendid portraitures of high conceptions, unbounded views, illimitable ardour, indomitable decision, and even when the event is mainly anti-prosperous to the high-toned machinations of the prime character, the potent, pervading hero of the story, it leaves us full of generous emotions for him, our hearts are paralysed. 'Twere pseudo-philosophy to assert that we do not feel more enwrapped by the brilliancy of his career than by the tranquil and morbid virtues of any opposing character. Our approbation of the latter is but eleemosynary.[3] These are the novels which enlarge the primitive capabilities of the heart, and which it cannot impugn the sense or be any dereliction of the character, of the most anti-puerile man, to be conversant with.'

'If I understand you aright,' said Charlotte, 'our taste in novels is not at all the same.' And here they were obliged to part, Miss Denham being too much tired of them all to stay any longer.

The truth was that Sir Edward, whom circumstances had confined very much to one spot, had read more sentimental novels than agreed with him. His fancy had been early caught by all the impassioned, and most exceptionable parts of Richardson, and such authors as have since appeared to tread in Richardson's steps, so far as man's determined pursuit of woman in defiance of every opposition of feeling and convenience is concerned, had since occupied the greater part of his literary hours, and formed his character.[4] With a perversity of judgement, which must be attributed to his not having by nature a very strong head, the graces, the spirit, the sagacity and the perseverance of the villain of the story outweighed all his absurdities and all his atrocities with Sir Edward. With his, such conduct was genius, fire and feeling. It interested and inflamed him, and he was always more anxious for its success and mourned over its discomfitures with more tenderness than could ever have been contemplated by the authors.

Though he owed many of his ideas to this sort of reading, it were unjust to say that he read nothing else, or that his language were not formed on a more general knowledge of modern literature. He read all the essays, letters, tours and criticisms of the day, and with the same ill-luck which made him derive only false principles from lessons of morality, and incentives to vice from the history of its overthrow, he gathered only hard words and involved sentences from the style of our most approved writers.

Sir Edward's great object in life was to be seductive. With such personal advantages as he knew himself to possess, and such talents as he did also give himself credit for, he regarded it as his duty. He felt that he was formed to be a dangerous man, quite in the line of the Lovelaces. The very name of Sir Edward, he thought, carried some degree of fascination with it. To be generally gallant and assiduous about the fair, to make fine speeches to every pretty girl, was but the inferior part of the character he had to play. Miss Heywood, or any other young woman with any pretensions to beauty, he was entitled (according to his own views of society) to approach with high compliments and rhapsody on the slightest acquaintance, but it was Clara alone on whom he had serious designs; it was Clara whom he meant to seduce. Her seduction was quite determined on. Her situation in every way called for it. She was his rival in Lady Denham's favour, she was young, lovely and dependant. He had very early seen the necessity of the case, and had now been long trying with cautious assiduity to make an impression on her heart, and to undermine her principles. Clara saw through him, and had not the least intention of being seduced, but she bore with him patiently enough to confirm the sort of attachment which her personal charms had raised.

A greater degree of discouragement indeed would not have affected Sir Edward. He was armed against the highest pitch of disdain or aversion. If she could not be won by affection, he must carry her off. He knew his business. Already he had many musings on the subject. If he were constrained to act, he must naturally wish to strike out something new, to exceed those who had gone before him, and he felt a strong curiosity to ascertain whether the neighbourhood of Timbuctoo might not afford some solitary house adapted for Clara's reception. But the expense, alas! of measures in that masterly style was ill-suited to his purse, and prudence obliged him to prefer the quietest sort of ruin and disgrace for the object of his affections, to the more renowned.

CHAPTER NINE

One day, soon after Charlotte's arrival at Sanditon, she had the pleasure of seeing, just as she ascended from the sands to the terrace, a gentleman's carriage with post-horses standing at the door of the hotel, as very lately arrived, and by the quantity of luggage taking off, bringing, it might be hoped, some respectable family determined on a long residence. Delighted to have such good news for Mr and Mrs Parker, who had both gone home some time before, she proceeded for Trafalgar House with as much alacrity as could remain after having been contending for the last two hours with a very fine wind blowing directly on shore, but she had not reached the little lawn when she saw a lady walking nimbly behind her at no great distance, and convinced that it could be no acquaintance of her own, she resolved to hurry on and get into the house if possible before her.

But the stranger's pace did not allow this to be accomplished, Charlotte was on the steps and had rung, but the door was not opened, when the other crossed the lawn, and when the servant appeared, they were just equally ready for entering the house. The ease of the lady, her, 'How do you do Morgan?' and Morgan's looks on seeing her were a moment's astonishment, but another moment brought Mr Parker into the hall to welcome the sister he had seen from the drawing room, and she was soon introduced to Miss Diana Parker. There was a great deal of surprise but still more pleasure in seeing her. Nothing could be kinder than her reception from both husband and wife.

'How did she come? And with whom?' They were so glad to find her equal to the journey! And that she was to belong to *them* was a thing of course. Mrs Diana Parker was about four and thirty, of middling height and slender, delicate looking rather than sickly, with an agreeable face and a very animated eye, her manners resembling her brother's in their ease and frankness, though with more decision and less mildness in her tone. She began an account of herself without delay, thanking them for their invitation, but '*that* was quite out of the question,' for they were all three come, and 'meant to get into lodgings and make some stay.'

'All three come! What? Susan able to come too?' This was better and better.

'Yes, we are actually all come. Quite unavoidable, nothing else to be done. You shall hear about it. But my dear Mary, send for the children, I long to see them.'

'And how has Susan borne the journey? And how is Arthur? And why do we not see him here with you?'

'Susan has borne it wonderfully. She had not a wink of sleep either the night before we set out, or last night at Chichester, and as this is not so common with her as with me, I have had a thousand fears for her, but she had kept up wonderfully, had no hysterics of consequence until we came within sight of poor old Sanditon, and the attack was not very violent, nearly over by the time we reached your hotel, so that we got her out of the carriage extremely well, with only Mr Woodcock's assistance. When I left her she was directing the disposal of the luggage and helping old Sam uncord the trunks. She desired her best love, with a thousand regrets at being so poor a creature that she could not come with me. And as for poor Arthur, he would not have been unwilling himself, but there is so much wind that I did not think he could safely venture, for I am sure there is lumbago hanging about him, so I helped him on with his greatcoat and sent him off to the terrace to take us lodgings. Miss Heywood must have seen our carriage standing at the hotel. I knew Miss Heywood the moment I saw her before me on the down. My dear Tom, I am so glad to see you walk so well. Let me feel your ankle. That's right, all right and clean. The play of your sinews a very little affected, barely perceptible. Well, now for the explanation of my being here. I told you in my letter of the two considerable families I was hoping to secure for you, the West Indians and the seminary.'[5]

Here Mr Parker drew his chair still nearer to his sister and took her hand again most affectionately as he answered, 'Yes, yes, how active and kind you have been!'

'The West Indians,' she continued, 'whom I look upon as the most desirable of the two, as the best of the good, prove to be a Mrs Griffiths and her family. I know them only through others. You must have heard me mention Miss Capper, the particular friend of my particular friend Fanny Noyce. Now, Miss Capper is extremely intimate with a Mrs Darling, who is on terms of constant correspondence with Mrs Griffiths herself. Only a short chain, you see, between us, and not a link wanting. Mrs Griffiths meant to go to the sea, for her young people's benefit, and had fixed upon Sussex, but was undecided as to the where, wanted something private, and wrote to ask the opinion of her friend Mrs Darling. Miss Capper happened to be staying with Mrs Darling when Mrs Griffith's letter arrived, and was consulted on the question; she wrote the same day to Fanny Noyce and mentioned it to her, and Fanny all alive for us, instantly took up her pen and forwarded the circumstance to me, except for the names, which have but lately transpired. There was but one thing for me to do. I answered Fanny's letter by the same post and pressed for the recommendation of Sanditon. Fanny had feared your having no house large enough to receive such a family. But I seem to be spinning out my story to an endless length. You see how it was all managed. I had the pleasure of hearing soon afterwards by the same link of connection that Sanditon had been recommended by Mrs Darling, and that the West Indians were very much disposed to go thither. This was the state of the case when I wrote to you, but two days ago, yes, the day before yesterday, I heard again from Fanny Noyce, saying she had heard from Mrs Capper, who by a letter from Mrs Darling understood that Mrs Griffiths has expressed herself in a letter to Mrs Darling more doubtingly on the subject of Sanditon. Am I clear? I would be anything rather than not clear.'

'Oh! Perfectly, perfectly. Well?'

'The reason of this hesitation, was her having no connections in the place, and no means of ascertaining that she should have good accommodations on arriving there, and she was particularly careful and scrupulous on all those matters more on account of a certain Miss Lambe, a young lady (probably a niece) under her care, than on her own account or her daughter's. Miss Lambe has an immense fortune, richer than all the rest, and very delicate health. One sees clearly enough by all this, the sort of woman Mrs Griffiths must be, as helpless and indolent as wealth and a hot climate are apt to make us. But we are not all born to equal energy. What was to be done? I had a few moments' indecision, whether to write to you or to Mrs Whitby to secure them a house, but neither pleased me. I hate to employ others when I am equal to act myself, and my conscience told me that this was an occasion which called for me. Here was a family of helpless invalids whom I might essentially serve. I sounded Susan – the same thought had occurred to her. Arthur made no difficulties, our plan was arranged immediately, we were off yesterday morning at six, left Chichester at the same hour today, and here we are.'

'Excellent, excellent!' cried Mr Parker. 'Diana, you are unequalled in serving your friends and doing good to all the world. I know nobody like you. Mary, my love, is she not a wonderful creature? Well, and now, what house do you design to engage for them? What is the size of their family?'

'I do not at all know,' replied his sister, 'have not the least idea, never heard any particulars, but I am sure that the largest at Sanditon cannot be too large. They are more likely to want a second. I shall take only one however, and that but for a week certain. Miss Heywood, I astonish you. You hardly know what to make of me. I see by your looks that you are not used to such quick measures.'

The words, 'Unaccountable officiousness! Activity run mad!' had just passed through Charlotte's mind, but a civil answer was easy.

'I do say I do look surprised,' said she, 'because these are very great exertions, and I know what invalids both you and your sister are.'

'Invalids indeed. I trust there are not three people in England who have so sad a right to that appellation! But my dear Miss Heywood, we are sent into this world, and where some degree of strength of mind is given, it is not a feeble body which will excuse us or incline us to excuse ourselves. The world is pretty much divided between the weak of mind and the strong, between those who can act and those who cannot, and it is the bounden duty of the capable to let no opportunity of being useful escape them. My sister's complaints and mine are happily not often of a nature to threaten existence immediately, and as long as we can exert ourselves to be of use to others, I am convinced that the body is the better for the refreshment the mind receives in doing its duty. While I have been travelling, with this object in view, I have been perfectly well.'

The entrance of the children ended this little panegyric on her own disposition, and after having noticed and caressed them all, she prepared to go. 'Cannot you dine with us? Is not it possible to prevail on you to dine with us?' was then the cry, and that being absolutely negatived, it was, 'And when shall we see you again? And how can we be of use to you?', and Mr Parker warmly offered his assistance in taking the house for Mrs Griffiths.

'I will come to you the moment I have dined,' said he, 'and we will go about it together.' But this was immediately declined.

'No, my dear Tom, upon no account in the world shall you stir a step on any business of mine. Your ankle wants rest. I see by the position of your foot that you have used it too much already. No, I shall go about my house-taking directly. Our dinner is not ordered until six, and by that time I hope to have completed it. It is now only half past four. As to seeing me again today, I cannot answer for it; the others will be at the hotel all evening, and delighted to see you at any time, but as soon as I get back I shall hear what Arthur has done about our own lodgings, and probably the moment dinner is over, shall be out again on business relative to them, for we hope to get into some lodgings or other and be settled after breakfast tomorrow. I have not much confidence in poor Arthur's skill for lodging-taking, but he seemed to like the commission.'

'I think you are doing too much,' said Mr Parker, 'You will knock yourself up. You should not move again after dinner.'

'No, indeed you should not,' cried his wife, 'for dinner is such a mere name with you all, that it can do you no good. I know what your appetites are.'

'My appetite is very much mended, I assure you, lately. I have been taking some bitters of my own decocting, which have done wonders. Susan never eats, I grant you – and just at present I shall want nothing, I never eat for about a week after a journey; but as for Arthur, he is only too much disposed for food. We are often obliged to check him.'

'But you have not told me anything of the other family coming to Sanditon,' said Mr Parker as he walked with her to the door of the house, 'the Camberwell seminary, have we a good chance of them?'

'Oh! Certain, quite certain. I had forgotten them for the moment, but I had a letter three days ago from my friend Mrs Charles Dupuis which assured me of Camberwell. Camberwell will be here to a certainty, and very soon. That good woman (I do not know her name) not being so wealthy and independent as Mrs Griffiths, can travel and choose for herself. I will tell you how I got at her. Mrs Charles Dupuis lives almost next door to a lady, who has a relation lately settled at Clapham, who actually attends the seminary and gives lessons on eloquence and *belles lettres* to some of the girls. I got that man a hare from one of Sidney's friends, and he recommended Sanditon. Without my appearing however, Mrs Charles Dupuis managed it all.'

CHAPTER TEN

It was not a week since Miss Diana Parker had been told by her feelings that the sea air would probably, in her present state, be the death of her, and now she was at Sanditon, intending to make some stay without appearing to have the slightest recollection of having written or felt any such thing. It was impossible for Charlotte not to suspect a good deal of fancy in such an extraordinary state of health. Disorders and recoveries so very much out of the way, seemed more like the amusement of eager minds in want of employment than of actual afflictions and relief. The Parkers were no doubt a family of imagination and quick feelings, and while the eldest brother found vent for his superfluity of sensation as a projector, the sisters were perhaps driven to dissipate theirs in the invention of odd complaints. The *whole* of their mental vivacity was evidently not so employed; part was laid out in a zeal for being useful. It should seem that they must either be very busy for the good of others, or else extremely ill themselves. Some natural delicacy of constitution in fact, with an unfortunate turn for medicine, especially quack medicine, had given them an early tendency at various times to various disorders; the rest of their sufferings were from fancy, the love of distinction and the love of the wonderful. They had charitable hearts and many amiable feelings, but a spirit of restless activity and the glory of doing more than anybody else, had their share in every exertion of benevolence, and there was vanity in all they did as well as in all they endured.

Mr and Mrs Parker spent a great part of the evening at the hotel, but Charlotte had only two or three views of Miss Diana posting over the down after a house for this lady whom she had never seen and who had never employed her. She was not made acquainted with the others until the following day, when, being removed into lodgings and all the party continuing quite well, their mother and sister and herself were entreated to drink tea with them. They were in one of the terrace houses, and she found them arranged for the evening in a small neat drawing room, with a beautiful view of the sea if they had chosen it, but though it had been a very fair English summer day, not only was there no open window, but the sofa and the table and the establishment in general was all at the other end of the room by a brisk fire. Miss Parker, whom, remembering the three teeth drawn in one day, Charlotte approached with a peculiar degree of respectful compassion, was not very unlike her sister in person or manner, though more thin and worn by illness and medicine, more relaxed in air and more subdued in voice. She talked, however, the whole evening as incessantly as Diana, and excepting that she sat with salts in her hand, took drops two or three times from one, out of the several phials already at home on the mantelpiece, and made a great many odd faces and contortions, Charlotte could perceive no symptoms of illness which she, in the boldness of her own good health, would not have undertaken to cure by putting out the fire, opening the window and disposing of the drops and the salts by means of one or the other. She had had considerable curiosity to see Mr Arthur Parker, and having fancied him a very puny, delicate-looking young man, the smallest very materially of not a robust family, was astonished to find him quite as tall as his brother and a good deal stouter, broad-made and lusty, and with no other look of an invalid than a sodden complexion.

Diana was evidently the chief of the family, principal mover and actor, she had been on her feet the whole morning, on Mrs Griffith's business or their own, and was still the most alert of the three. Susan had only superintended their final removal from the hotel, bringing two heavy boxes herself, and Arthur had found the air so cold that he had merely walked from one house to the other as nimbly as he could, and boasted much of sitting by the fire until he had cooked up a very good one. Diana, whose exercise had been too domestic to admit of calculation, but who, by her own account, had not once sat down during the space of seven hours, confessed herself a little tired. She had been too successful however for much fatigue, for not only had she by walking and talking down a thousand difficulties at last secured a proper house at eight guineas per week for Mrs Griffiths, she had opened so many treaties with cooks, housemaids, washer-women and bathing-women that Mrs Griffiths would have little more to do on her arrival than to wave her hand and collect them around her for choice. Her concluding effort in the cause had been a few polite lines of information to Mrs Griffiths herself – time not allowing for the circuitous train of intelligence, which had been hitherto kept up – and she was now regaling in the delight of opening the first trenches of an acquaintance with such a powerful discharge of unexpected obligation.

Mr and Mrs Parker, and Charlotte, had seen two post-chaises crossing the down to the hotel as they were setting off – a joyful sight, and full of speculation. The Miss Parkers and Arthur had also seen something, they could distinguish from their window that there was an arrival at the hotel, but not its amount. Their visitors answered for two hack-chaises. Could it be the Camberwell seminary? No, no. Had there been a third carriage, perhaps it might, but it was very generally agreed that two hack-chaises could never contain a seminary. Mr Parker was confident of another new family.

When they were all finally seated, after some removals to look at the sea and the hotel, Charlotte's place was by Arthur, who was sitting next to the fire with a degree of enjoyment which gave a good deal of merit to his civility in wishing her to take his chair. There was nothing dubious in her manner of declining it, and he sat down again with much satisfaction. She drew back her chair to have all the advantage of his person as a screen, and was very thankful for every inch of back and shoulders beyond her preconceived idea. Arthur was heavy in eye as will as figure, but by no means indisposed to talk, and while the other four were chiefly engaged together, he evidently felt it no penance to have a fine young woman next to him, requiring in common politeness some attention, as his brother, who felt the decided want of some motive for action, some powerful object of animation for him, observed with considerable pleasure.

Such was the influence of youth and bloom that he began even to make a sort of apology for having a fire. 'We should not have one at home,' said he, 'but the sea air is always damp. I am not afraid of anything so much as damp.'

'I am so fortunate,' said Charlotte, 'as never to know whether the air is damp or dry. It has always some property that is wholesome and invigorating to me.'

'I like the air too, as well as anybody can,' replied Arthur, 'I am very fond of standing at an open window when there is no wind, but unluckily a damp air does not like me. It gives me the rheumatism. You are not rheumatic, I suppose?'

'Not at all.'

'That's a great blessing. But perhaps you are nervous?'

'No, I believe not. I have no idea what I am.'

'I am very nervous. To say the truth, nerves are the worst part of my complaints in my opinion. My sisters think me bilious, but I doubt it.'

'You are quite in the right, to doubt it as long as you possibly can, I am sure.'

'If I were bilious,' he continued, 'you know wine would disagree with me, but it always does me good. The more wine I drink (in moderation), the better I am. I am always best of an evening. If you had seen me today before dinner, you would have thought me a very poor creature.'

Charlotte could believe it. She kept her countenance however, and said, 'As far as I can understand what nervous complaints are, I have a great idea of the efficacy of air and exercise for them; daily, regular exercise. I should recommend rather more of it to you than I suspect you are in the habit of taking.'

'Oh! I am very fond of exercise myself,' he replied, 'and mean to walk a great deal while I am here, if the weather is temperate. I shall be out every morning before breakfast, and take several turns upon the terrace, and you will often see me at Trafalgar House.'

'But you do not call a walk to Trafalgar House much exercise?'

'Not as to mere distance, but the hill is so steep! Walking up that hill in the middle of the day would throw me into such a perspiration! You would see me all in a bath by the time I got there! I am very subject to perspiration, and there cannot be a surer sign of nervousness.'

They were now advancing so deep in physics that Charlotte viewed the entrance of the servant with the tea things as a very fortunate interruption. It produced a great and immediate change. The young man's attentions were instantly lost. He took his own cocoa from the tray, which seemed provided with almost as many teapots as there were persons in company, Miss Parker drinking one sort of herb tea and Miss Diana another, and turning completely to the fire, sat coddling and cooking it to his own satisfaction and toasting some slices of bread, brought up ready-prepared in the toastrack, and until it was done, she heard nothing of his voice but the murmuring of a few broken sentences of self-approbation and success.

When his toils were over however, he moved back his chair into as gallant a line as ever, and proved that he had not been working only for himself, by his earnest invitation to Charlotte to take both cocoa and toast. She was already helped to tea, which surprised him, so totally self-engrossed he had been. 'I thought I should have been in time,' said he, 'but cocoa takes a great deal of boiling.'

'I am much obliged to you,' replied Charlotte, 'but I prefer tea.'

'Then I will help myself,' said he. 'A large dish of rather weak cocoa every evening agrees with me better than anything.' It struck her however, as he poured out this rather weak cocoa, that it came forth in a very fine, dark-coloured stream, and at the same moment, his sisters both crying out:

'Oh! Arthur, you get your cocoa stronger and stronger every evening!' with Arthur's somewhat conscious reply of:

"*Tis* rather stronger than it should be tonight,' convinced her that Arthur was by no means so fond of being starved as they could desire, or as he felt proper himself. He was certainly very happy to turn the conversation on dry toast, and hear no more of his sisters. 'I hope you will eat some of this toast,' said he, 'I reckon myself a very good toaster, I never burn my toasts, I never put them too near the fire at first, and yet, you see, there is not a corner but what is well browned. I hope you like dry toast.'

'With a reasonable quantity of butter spread over it, very much,' said Charlotte, 'but not otherwise.'

'No more do I,' said he, exceedingly pleased, 'we think quite alike there. So far from dry toast being wholesome, I think it is a very bad thing for the stomach. Without a little butter to soften it, it hurts the coats of the stomach. I am sure it does. I will have the pleasure of spreading some for you directly, and afterwards I will spread some for myself. Very bad indeed for the coats of the stomach, but there is no convincing some people. It irritates and acts like a nutmeg grater.' He could not get command of the butter, however, without a struggle, his sisters accusing him of eating a great deal too much, and declaring he was not to be trusted, and he maintaining that he only ate enough to secure the coats of his stomach, and besides, he only wanted it now for Miss Heywood. Such a plea must prevail, he got the butter and spread away for her with an accuracy of judgement which at least delighted himself, but when her toast was done, and he took his own in hand, Charlotte could hardly contain herself as she saw him watching his sisters, while he scrupulously scraped off almost as much better as he put on, and then seize an odd moment for adding a great dab just before it went into his mouth.

Certainly, Mr Arthur Parker's enjoyments in invalidism were very different from his sisters' – by no means so spiritualised. A good deal of earthly dross hung about him. Charlotte could not but suspect him of adopting that line of life, principally for the indulgence of an indolent temper, and to be determined on having no disorders but such as called for warm rooms and good nourishment. In one particular however, she soon found that he had caught something from them.

'What!' said he, 'Do you venture upon two dishes of strong green tea in one evening? What nerves you must have! How I envy you. Now, if I were to swallow only one such dish, what do you think its effect would be upon me?'

'Keep you awake perhaps all night?' replied Charlotte, meaning to overthrow his attempts at surprise by the grandeur of her own conceptions.

'Oh! If that were all!' he exclaimed. 'No, it acts upon me like poison and would entirely take away the use of my right side, before I had swallowed it five minutes. It sounds almost incredible but it has happened to me so often that I cannot doubt it. The use of my right side is entirely taken away for several hours!'

'It sounds rather odd to be sure,' answered Charlotte coolly, 'but I dare say it would be proved to be the simplest thing in the world by those who have studied right sides and green tea scientifically and thoroughly understand all the possibilities of their action on each other.'

Soon after tea, a letter was brought to Miss Diana Parker from the hotel. 'From Mrs Charles Dupuis,' said she, 'some private hand.' And having read a few lines, exclaimed aloud, 'Well, this is very extraordinary! Very extraordinary indeed! That both should have the same name. Two Mrs Griffiths! This is a letter of recommendation and introduction to me, of the lady from Camberwell, and her name happens to be Griffiths too!' A few lines more, however, and the colour rushed into her cheeks, and with much perturbation she added, 'the oddest thing that ever was! A Miss Lambe too! A young West Indian of large fortune. But it cannot be the same. Impossible that it should be the same.' She read the letter aloud for comfort. It was merely to 'introduce the bearer, Mrs Griffiths from Camberwell, and the three young ladies under her care, to Miss Diana Parker's notice. Mrs Griffiths, being a stranger at Sanditon, was anxious for a respectable introduction, and Mrs Charles Dupuis therefore, at the instance of the intermediate friend, provided her with this letter, knowing that she could not do her dear Diana a greater kindness than by giving her the means of being useful. Mrs Griffiths' chief solicitude would be for the accommodation and comfort of one of the ladies under her care, a Miss Lambe, a young West Indian of large fortune, in delicate health.'

It was 'very strange!', 'very remarkable!', 'very extraordinary!', but they were all agreed in determining it to be impossible that there should not be two families, such a totally distinct set of people as were concerned in the reports of each made that matter quite certain. There must be two families. 'Impossible' and 'Impossible' was repeated over and over again with great fervour. An accidental resemblance of names and circumstances, however striking at first, involved nothing really incredible, and so it was settled. Miss Diana herself derived an immediate advantage to counterbalance her perplexity. She must put her shawl over her shoulders, and be running about again. Tired as she was, she must instantly repair to the hotel, to investigate the truth and offer her services.

CHAPTER ELEVEN

It would not do. Nothing that the whole Parker race could say among themselves could produce a happier catastrophe than that the family from Surrey and the family from Camberwell were one and the same. The rich West Indians and the young ladies' seminary had all entered Sanditon in those two hack-chaises. The Mrs Griffiths who, in her friend Mrs Darling's hands, had wavered as to coming and been unequal to the journey, was the very same Mrs Griffiths whose plans were at the same period (under another representation) perfectly decided, and who was without fears or difficulties. All that had the appearance of incongruity in the reports of the two might very fairly be placed to the account of the vanity, the ignorance or the blunders of the many engaged in the cause by the vigilance and caution of Miss Diana Parker. Her intimate friends must be officious like herself, and the subject had supplied letters and extracts and messages enough to make everything appear what it was not.

Miss Diana probably felt a little awkward on being first obliged to admit her mistake. A long journey from Hampshire taken for nothing, a brother disappointed, and an expensive house on her hands for a week must have been some of her immediate reflections, and much worse than all the rest must have been the sort of sensation of being less clear-sighted and infallible than she had believed herself. No part of it however seemed to trouble her long. There were so many to share in the shame and the blame that probably when she had divided out their proper portions to Mrs Darling, Capper, Fanny Noyce, Mrs Charles Dupuis and Mrs Charles Dupuis' neighbour, there might be a mere trifle of reproach remaining for herself. At any rate, she was seen all the following morning walking about after lodgings with Mrs Griffiths, as alert as ever.

Mrs Griffiths was a very well-behaved, genteel kind of woman, who supported herself by receiving such great girls and young ladies, as wanted either masters for finishing their education or a home for beginning their displays. She had several more under her care than the three who were now come to Sanditon, but the others all happened to be absent. Of these three, and indeed of all, Miss Lambe was beyond comparison the most important and precious, as she paid in proportion to her fortune. She was about seventeen, half mulatto,[6] chilly and tender, had a maid of her own, was to have the best room in the lodgings, and was always of the first consequence in every plan of Mrs Griffiths.

The other girls, two Miss Beauforts, were just such young ladies as may be met with, in at least one family out of three throughout the kingdom. They had tolerable complexions, showy figures, an upright decided carriage and an assured look. They were very accomplished and very ignorant; their time being divided between such pursuits as might attract admiration, and those labours and expedients of dexterous ingenuity by which they could dress in a style much beyond what they ought to have afforded. They were some of the very first in every change of fashion, and the object of all was to captivate some man of much better fortune than their own.

Mrs Griffiths had preferred a small, retired place like Sanditon on Miss Lambe's account, and the Miss Beauforts, though naturally preferring anything to smallness and retirement and having in the course of the spring been involved in the inevitable expense of six new dresses each for a three-day visit, were constrained to be satisfied with Sanditon also, until their circumstances were retrieved. There, with the hire of a harp for one, and the purchase of some drawing paper for the other and all the finery they could already command, they meant to be very economical, very elegant and very secluded, with the hope on Miss Beaufort's side of praise and celebrity from all who walked within the sound of her instrument, and on Miss Letitia's of curiosity and rapture in all who came near her while she sketched, and to both, the consolation of meaning to be the most stylish girls in the place.

The particular introduction of Mrs Griffiths to Miss Diana Parker secured them immediately an acquaintance with the Trafalgar House family and with the Denhams, and the Miss Beauforts were soon satisfied with 'the circle in which they moved in Sanditon', to use a proper phrase, for everybody must now 'move in a circle', to the prevalence of which rotary motion is perhaps to be attributed the giddiness and false steps of many.

Lady Denham had other motives for calling on Mrs Griffiths besides attention to the Parkers. In Miss Lambe, here was the very young lady, sickly and rich, whom she had been asking for, and she made the acquaintance for Sir Edward's sake, and the sake of her milch asses. How it might answer with regard to the baronet remained to be proved, but as to the animals, she soon found that all her calculations of profit would be vain. Mrs Griffiths would not allow Miss Lambe to have the smallest symptom of a decline, or any complaint which asses' milk could possibly relieve. 'Miss Lambe was under the constant care of an experienced physician, and his prescriptions must be their rule', and except in favour of some tonic pills, which a cousin of her own had a property in, Mrs Griffiths did never deviate from the strict medicinal page.

The corner house of the terrace was the one in which Miss Diana Parker had the pleasure of settling her new friends, and considering that it commanded in front the favourite lounge of all the visitors at Sanditon, and on one side, whatever might be going on at the hotel, there could not have been a more favourable spot for the seclusions of the Miss Beauforts. Accordingly, long before they had suited themselves with an instrument or with drawing paper, they had, by the frequency of their appearance at the low windows upstairs, in order to close the blinds, or open the blinds, to arrange a flower pot on the balcony or look at nothing through a telescope, attracted many an eye upwards and made many a gazer gaze again. A little novelty has a great effect in so small a place, and the Beauforts, who would have been nothing at Brighton, could not move here without notice. Even Mr Arthur Parker, though little disposed for supernumerary exertion, always quitted the terrace, in his way to his brother's, by this corner house, for the sake of a glimpse of the Miss Beauforts, though it was half a quarter of a mile round about and added two steps to the ascent of the hill.

CHAPTER TWELVE

Charlotte had been ten days at Sanditon without seeing Sanditon House, every attempt at calling on Lady Denham having been defeated by meeting with her beforehand. But now it was to be more resolutely undertaken, at a more early hour, that nothing might be neglected of attention to Lady Denham or amusement to Charlotte. 'And if you should mean to find a favourable opening, my love,' said Mr Parker (who did not mean to go with them), 'I think you had better mention the poor Mullins' situation, and sound her Ladyship as to a subscription for them. I am not fond of charitable subscriptions in a place of this kind; it is a sort of tax upon all that come. Yet as their distress is very great and I almost promised the poor woman yesterday to get something done for her, I believe we must set a subscription on foot, and therefore the sooner the better, and Lady Denham's name at the head of the list will be a very necessary beginning. You will not dislike speaking to her about it, Mary?'

'I will do whatever you wish me,' replied his wife, 'but you would do it so much better yourself. I shall not know what to say.'

'My dear Mary,' cried he, 'it is impossible you can really be at a loss. Nothing can be more simple. You have only to state the present afflicted situation of the family, their earnest application to me, and my being willing to promote a little subscription for their relief, provided it meet with her approbation.'

'The easiest thing in the world,' cried Miss Diana Parker, who happened to be calling on them at the moment, 'all said and done, in less time than you have been talking of it now. And while you are on the subject of subscriptions, Mary, I will thank you to mention a very melancholy case to Lady Denham which has been represented to me in the most affecting terms. There is a poor woman in Worcestershire, whom some friends of mine are exceedingly interested about, and I have undertaken to collect whatever I can for her. If you would, mention the circumstance to Lady Denham! Lady Denham can give, if she is properly attacked, and I look upon her to be the sort of person who, when once she is prevailed upon to undraw her purse, would as readily give ten guineas as five. And therefore, if you would find her in a giving mood, you might as well speak in favour of another charity which I and a few more have very much at heart, the establishment of a charitable responsibility at Burton-on-Trent. And then, there is the family of the poor man who was hung last assizes at York, though we really have raised the sum we wanted for putting them all out, yet if you can get a guinea from her on their behalf, it may as well be done.'

'My dear Diana!' exclaimed Mrs Parker, 'I could no more mention these things to Lady Denham than I could fly.'

'Where's the difficulty? I wish I could go with you myself, but in five minutes I must be at Mrs Griffiths' to encourage Miss Lambe in taking her first dip. She is so frightened, poor thing, that I promised to come and keep up her spirits, and go in the machine with her if she wished it, and as soon as that is over, I must hurry home, for Susan is to have leeches at one o'clock, which will be a three-hour business, therefore I really have not a moment to spare, besides that (between ourselves), I ought to be in bed myself at this present time, for I am hardly able to stand, and when the leeches have done, I dare say we shall both go to our rooms for the rest of the day.'

'I am sorry to hear it, indeed, but if this is the case I hope Arthur will come to us.'

'If Arthur takes my advice, he will go to bed too, for if he stays up by himself, he will certainly eat and drink more than he ought; but you see Mary, how impossible it is for me to go with you to Lady Denham's.'

'Upon second thoughts, Mary,' said her husband, 'I will not trouble you to speak about the Mullins. I will take an opportunity of seeing Lady Denham myself. I know how little it suits you to be pressing matters upon a mind at all unwilling.'

His application thus withdrawn, his sister could say no more in support of hers, which was his object, as he felt all their impropriety and all the certainty of their ill effect upon his own better claim. Mrs Parker was delighted at this release, and set off very happy with her friend and her little girl on this walk to Sanditon House. It was a close, misty morning, and when they reached the brow of the hill, they could not for some time make out what sort of carriage it was, which they saw coming up. It appeared at different moments to be everything from the gig to the phaeton, from one horse to four, and just as they were concluding in favour of a tandem, little Mary's young eyes distinguished the coachman and she eagerly called out, "'Tis Uncle Sidney, mama, it is indeed!' And so it proved. Mr Sidney Parker driving his servant in a very neat carriage was soon opposite to them, and they all stopped for a few minutes. The manners of the Parkers were always pleasant among themselves, and it was a very friendly meeting between Sidney and his sister-in-law, who was most kindly taking it for granted that he was on his was to Trafalgar House. This he declined, however.

'He was just come up from Eastbourne, proposing to spend two or three days, as it might happen, at Sanditon, but the hotel must be his quarters. He was expecting to be joined there by a friend or two.' The rest was common enquiries and remarks, with kind notice of little Mary, and a very well-bred bow and proper address to Miss Heywood on her being named to him, and they parted, to meet again within a few hours. Sidney Parker was about seven or eight and twenty, very good-looking, with a decided air of ease and fashion, and a lively countenance. This adventure afforded agreeable discussion for some time. Mrs Parker entered into all her husband's joy on the occasion, and exulted in the credit which Sidney's arrival would give to the place.

The road to Sanditon House was a broad, handsome, planted approach, between fields, and conducting at the end of a quarter of a mile through second gates into the grounds, which though not extensive had all the beauty and respect-ability which an abundance of very fine timber could give. These entrance gates were so much in a corner of the grounds, or paddock, so near one of its boundaries, that an outside fence was at first almost pressing on the road, until an angle here and a curve there threw them to a better distance. The fence was a proper park paling in excellent condition, with clusters of fine elms or rows of old thorns following its line almost everywhere.

'Almost' must be stipulated, for there were vacant spaces, and through one of these, as soon as they entered the enclos-ure, Charlotte caught a glimpse over the pales of something white and womanish in the field on the other side; it was something which immediately brought Miss Brereton into her head, and stepping to the pales, she saw indeed, and very decidedly, in spite of the mist, Miss Brereton, seated, not far before her, at the foot of the bank which sloped down from the outside of the paling, and which a narrow path seemed to skirt along. Miss Brereton was seated apparently very composedly, with Sir Edward Denham by her side. They were sitting so near each other and appeared so closely engaged in gentle conversation that Charlotte instantly felt she had nothing to do but step back again, and say not a word. Privacy was certainly their object. It could not but strike her rather unfavourably with regard to Clara, but hers was a situation which must not be judged with severity.

She was glad to perceive that nothing had been discerned by Mrs Parker. If Charlotte had not been considerably the taller of the two, Miss Brereton's white ribbons might not have fallen within the ken of her more observant eyes. Among other points of moralising reflection which the sight of this tête-à-tête produced, Charlotte could not but think of the extreme difficulty which secret lovers must have in finding a proper spot for their stolen interviews. Here, perhaps, they had thought themselves so perfectly secure from observation, the whole field open before them, a steep bank and pales never crossed by the foot of man at their back, and a great thickness of air, in their aid. Yet here, she had seen them. They were really ill-used.

The house was large and handsome; two servants appeared, to admit them, and everything had a suitable air of property and order. Lady Denham valued herself upon her liberal establishment, and had great enjoyment in the order and the importance of her style of living. They were shown into the usual sitting room, well proportioned and well furnished, though it was furniture rather originally good and extremely well kept, rather than new or showy, and as Lady Denham was not there, Charlotte had leisure to look about, and to be told by Mrs Parker that the whole-length portrait of a stately gentleman, placed over the mantelpiece, was the picture of Sir Harry Denham, and that one among many miniatures in another part of the room, little conspicuous, represented Mr Hollis. Poor Mr Hollis! It was impossible not to feel him hardly used, to be obliged to stand back in his own house and see the best place by the fire constantly occupied by Sir Harry Denham.

NOTES

1. A picturesque, rustic dwelling then popular among members of the fashionable classes keen to demonstrate their affinity with nature.

2. A novel by Fanny Burney, published in 1796. Its subtitle is 'A Picture of Youth'.

3. Charitable.

4. Richardson's *Clarissa* (1748–9) recounts the story of a virtuous young woman whose family attempt to trick her into marriage, and who is then abducted and raped by the young aristocrat Lovelace.

5. A private school.

6. A person who has one black and one white parent.

BIOGRAPHICAL NOTE

Jane Austen was born in 1775 in Steventon, Hampshire, the seventh of eight children. Her father, the Revd George Austen, was a well-read and cultured man, and Jane was mostly educated at home. She read voraciously as a child, in particular the works of Fielding, Sterne, Richardson and Scott. She also began writing at a very young age, producing her earliest work when she was just twelve years old.

On her father's death in 1805, Austen and her mother moved to Southampton. They then settled in Chawton, Hampshire, in 1819, and it was here that her major novels were written. Despite leading a remarkably uneventful life herself – she never married, and seldom left home – her works are noted for her incredible powers of observation. Only four novels were published during her lifetime – *Sense and Sensibility* (1811), *Pride and Prejudice* (1813), *Mansfield Park* (1814) and *Emma* (1816) – and all were published anonymously. On a rare visit from home, she was taken ill, and she died from Addison's disease in 1817. Two further novels, *Persuasion* and *Northanger Abbey*, were published posthumously in 1818. *Sanditon* appeared in 1925.

SELECTED TITLES FROM HESPERUS PRESS

Author	Title	Foreword writer
Pietro Aretino	*The School of Whoredom*	Paul Bailey
Pietro Aretino	*The Secret Life of Nuns*	
Jane Austen	*Lesley Castle*	Zoë Heller
Jane Austen	*Love and Friendship*	Fay Weldon
Honoré de Balzac	*Colonel Chabert*	A.N. Wilson
Charles Baudelaire	*On Wine and Hashish*	Margaret Drabble
Giovanni Boccaccio	*Life of Dante*	A.N. Wilson
Charlotte Brontë	*The Spell*	
Emily Brontë	*Poems of Solitude*	Helen Dunmore
Mikhail Bulgakov	*Fatal Eggs*	Doris Lessing
Mikhail Bulgakov	*The Heart of a Dog*	A.S. Byatt
Giacomo Casanova	*The Duel*	Tim Parks
Miguel de Cervantes	*The Dialogue of the Dogs*	Ben Okri
Geoffrey Chaucer	*The Parliament of Birds*	
Anton Chekhov	*The Story of a Nobody*	Louis de Bernières
Anton Chekhov	*Three Years*	William Fiennes
Wilkie Collins	*The Frozen Deep*	
Joseph Conrad	*Heart of Darkness*	A.N. Wilson
Joseph Conrad	*The Return*	Colm Tóibín
Gabriele D'Annunzio	*The Book of the Virgins*	Tim Parks
Dante Alighieri	*The Divine Comedy: Inferno*	
Dante Alighieri	*New Life*	Louis de Bernières
Daniel Defoe	*The King of Pirates*	Peter Ackroyd
Marquis de Sade	*Incest*	Janet Street-Porter
Charles Dickens	*The Haunted House*	Peter Ackroyd
Charles Dickens	*A House to Let*	
Fyodor Dostoevsky	*The Double*	Jeremy Dyson
Fyodor Dostoevsky	*Poor People*	Charlotte Hobson
Alexandre Dumas	*One Thousand and One Ghosts*	

George Eliot	*Amos Barton*	Matthew Sweet
Henry Fielding	*Jonathan Wild the Great*	Peter Ackroyd
F. Scott Fitzgerald	*The Popular Girl*	Helen Dunmore
Gustave Flaubert	*Memoirs of a Madman*	Germaine Greer
Ugo Foscolo	*Last Letters of Jacopo Ortis*	Valerio Massimo Manfredi
Elizabeth Gaskell	*Lois the Witch*	Jenny Uglow
Théophile Gautier	*The Jinx*	Gilbert Adair
André Gide	*Theseus*	
Johann Wolfgang von Goethe	*The Man of Fifty*	A.S. Byatt
Nikolai Gogol	*The Squabble*	Patrick McCabe
E.T.A. Hoffmann	*Mademoiselle de Scudéri*	Gilbert Adair
Victor Hugo	*The Last Day of a Condemned Man*	Libby Purves
Joris-Karl Huysmans	*With the Flow*	Simon Callow
Henry James	*In the Cage*	Libby Purves
Franz Kafka	*Metamorphosis*	Martin Jarvis
Franz Kafka	*The Trial*	Zadie Smith
John Keats	*Fugitive Poems*	Andrew Motion
Heinrich von Kleist	*The Marquise of O–*	Andrew Miller
Mikhail Lermontov	*A Hero of Our Time*	Doris Lessing
Nikolai Leskov	*Lady Macbeth of Mtsensk*	Gilbert Adair
Carlo Levi	*Words are Stones*	Anita Desai
Xavier de Maistre	*A Journey Around my Room*	Alain de Botton
André Malraux	*The Way of the Kings*	Rachel Seiffert
Katherine Mansfield	*Prelude*	William Boyd
Edgar Lee Masters	*Spoon River Anthology*	Shena Mackay
Guy de Maupassant	*Butterball*	Germaine Greer
Prosper Mérimée	*Carmen*	Philip Pullman
Sir Thomas More	*The History of King Richard III*	Sister Wendy Beckett
Sándor Petőfi	*John the Valiant*	George Szirtes

Francis Petrarch	*My Secret Book*	Germaine Greer
Luigi Pirandello	*Loveless Love*	
Edgar Allan Poe	*Eureka*	Sir Patrick Moore
Alexander Pope	*The Rape of the Lock and A Key to the Lock*	Peter Ackroyd
Antoine-François Prévost	*Manon Lescaut*	Germaine Greer
Marcel Proust	*Pleasures and Days*	A.N. Wilson
Alexander Pushkin	*Dubrovsky*	Patrick Neate
Alexander Pushkin	*Ruslan and Lyudmila*	Colm Tóibín
François Rabelais	*Pantagruel*	Paul Bailey
François Rabelais	*Gargantua*	Paul Bailey
Christina Rossetti	*Commonplace*	Andrew Motion
George Sand	*The Devil's Pool*	Victoria Glendinning
Jean-Paul Sartre	*The Wall*	Justin Cartwright
Friedrich von Schiller	*The Ghost-seer*	Martin Jarvis
Mary Shelley	*Transformation*	
Percy Bysshe Shelley	*Zastrozzi*	Germaine Greer
Stendhal	*Memoirs of an Egotist*	Doris Lessing
Robert Louis Stevenson	*Dr Jekyll and Mr Hyde*	Helen Dunmore
Theodor Storm	*The Lake of the Bees*	Alan Sillitoe
Leo Tolstoy	*The Death of Ivan Ilych*	
Leo Tolstoy	*Hadji Murat*	Colm Tóibín
Ivan Turgenev	*Faust*	Simon Callow
Mark Twain	*The Diary of Adam and Eve*	John Updike
Mark Twain	*Tom Sawyer, Detective*	
Oscar Wilde	*The Portrait of Mr W.H.*	Peter Ackroyd
Virginia Woolf	*Carlyle's House and Other Sketches*	Doris Lessing
Virginia Woolf	*Monday or Tuesday*	Scarlett Thomas
Emile Zola	*For a Night of Love*	A.N. Wilson

Warwickshire County Council

Working for Warwickshire

Discover ● Imagine ● Learn ● *with libraries*

● Visit www.warwickshire.gov.uk/libraries
● Phone the 24/7 Renewal Line 01926 499273 or
To renew your books: if not in demand. period
latest date above. It may be borrowed for a further
This item is to be returned or renewed before the

22.8.19
24/10/19
16. SEP. 10.

17. MAR

Warwickshire County Council